**"What are y**
**Why have**

He stared at her with those blue eyes that used to make her adolescent knees weak. "I heard about the old lighthouse being for sale. I'm thinking about making an offer."

Jenna's heart tripped. She closed her eyes. She couldn't look at his handsome face, so like his father's.

The son of the man who had killed her father was planning to buy the lighthouse.

Dear Reader,

This book is about a special place that reconnects two people with their past. In life, a location can evoke powerful emotions, both good and bad. For Nate Shelton, coming home to Finnegan Cove after twenty years, the lighthouse on the shore of Lake Michigan brings back memories of peace in his troubled youth and a hope for his family's future. But to Jenna Malloy, who never left the small town, the station has been a constant haunting memory of a tragedy from years ago that changed both characters' lives forever. Now the decaying building houses secrets as dark as its abandoned beacon—secrets that could keep Jenna and Nate from forgiving past mistakes.

I hope you enjoy this story. And I hope you can tell that I love lighthouses. Proud structures with dozens of winding steps or small tokens that sit on a shelf, all kinds and sizes of lighthouses never fail to weave a spell of romance and mystery over me. And if, in your busy travels, you are lucky enough to pass a lighthouse, pull over, put on your comfortable shoes and circle your way to the top. The view is always worth the trip, just like the happy ending in a romance.

I love to hear from readers. You can visit my Web site at www.cynthiathomason.com, e-mail me at cynthoma@aol.com or write to me at P.O. Box 550068, Fort Lauderdale, FL 33355.

Happy reading,

*Cynthia Thomason*

# RETURN OF THE WILD SON

*Cynthia Thomason*

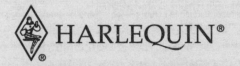

## HARLEQUIN®

TORONTO • NEW YORK • LONDON
AMSTERDAM • PARIS • SYDNEY • HAMBURG
STOCKHOLM • ATHENS • TOKYO • MILAN • MADRID
PRAGUE • WARSAW • BUDAPEST • AUCKLAND

ISBN-13: 978-0-373-71483-4
ISBN-10:  0-373-71483-1

RETURN OF THE WILD SON

This edition published by arrangement with Harlequin Books S.A.

® and TM are trademarks of the publisher. Trademarks indicated with ® are registered in the United States Patent and Trademark Office, the Canadian Trade Marks Office and in other countries.

www.eHarlequin.com

**Printed in U.S.A.**

# ABOUT THE AUTHOR

Cynthia Thomason writes contemporary and historical romances and dabbles in mysteries. When she's not writing, she works as a licensed auctioneer in the auction business she and her husband own. In this capacity, she has come across scores of unusual items, many of which have found their way into her books. She loves traveling the U.S. and exploring out-of-the-way places. She has one son, an entertainment reporter, and an aging but still lovable Jack Russell terrier. Cynthia dreams of perching on a mountaintop in North Carolina every autumn to watch the leaves turn. You can learn more about her at www.cynthiathomason.com.

## Books by Cynthia Thomason

### HARLEQUIN SUPERROMANCE

*Texas Hold 'Em

This book is dedicated to
my dearest climbing "Buddy," who has held my
hand on all the journeys we've taken together.
We haven't reached the top yet, and I believe
the last steps are the best.

# CHAPTER ONE

*Los Angeles, California*
*April*

NATE WALKED OUT OF Vincennti's and slipped the claim check for his BMW through the window of the valet hut. Carlo, who'd been parking cars here for as long as Nate had been coming to the renowned bistro, grabbed his keys from among dozens hanging on the board behind him and joined Nate in the sunshine.

"How was your lunch, Mr. Shelton?" he asked.

Seeing no point in answering truthfully, Nate swallowed the first symptom of indigestion and said, "Just fine, Carlo." He glanced nervously over his shoulder to the restaurant entrance. "I am kind of in a hurry, though."

"Sure, I understand. Isn't everybody in this town?" Carlo jogged across the circular drive, the keys jangling in his hand, and zigzagged through a maze of vehicles.

Nate needed Carlo to return with his car before Brendan Willis and his associate finished the last of their pricey merlot and came outside. It was bad enough that Nate had paid the hundred-and-fifty-dollar lunch tab. He didn't need another helping of condescension.

And he'd been so confident this time. He'd chosen Willis's Boneyard Films as the perfect production company for his latest screenplay after the big studios had turned him down. Boneyard's innovative producer was getting his name in print in *Variety* and *Entertainment Weekly*.

Still, Boneyard was a small independent, which meant Willis should have jumped at the chance to sign a Nathaniel Shelton script.

Now, an hour-and-a-half lunch later, Nate was fairly certain that even though the producer had agreed to read the script, their collaboration was going nowhere.

"I'll call you in a week or so," Brendan had said.

A week or so? Nate was used to getting offers an hour after dropping off his work. Of course, that was before he'd produced three flops in a row. But he was an award-winning writer, for Pete's sake, though most of the power brokers in this town seemed to have forgotten that accomplishment.

His steel-gray BMW pulled up to the curb and Carlo jumped out. "You have a good day, Mr. Shelton," he said. Nate pressed a modest tip in the guy's hand and drove off.

He headed toward his Beverly Hills condo. With the weekend ahead of him, he had to regroup, study the latest industry news journals and come up with another production company to pitch his latest project to. This was a big town, with countless possibilities, and Nate was a hell of a writer. No need to panic—yet.

The ringing of his cell phone jerked him back in his seat. He hit the speaker button and snapped, "Shelton."

"Nathaniel?"

At the sound of the gravelly voice, his heart constricted. "Dad? Is everything okay?"

"It's better than okay."

"Why, what's happened?"

"I didn't tell you before, son, because I didn't know what the parole board would decide."

"What are you talking about?" Nate's father had been incarcerated twenty years of a twenty-four-year sentence. Was parole possible this soon for a second-degree murder conviction? Nate knew his father had only been before the board one other time.

"I didn't get my hopes up," Harley said. "Guys are almost always flopped the first few times around."

Flopped. Prison talk for turned down. Nate had learned a lot of new meanings for old words since his father had been taken away. "Dad, what are you saying?"

"I'm going to be approved, Nate. Dr. Evanston told me a few minutes ago that I'm getting out May 23."

Nate's jaw dropped. He did a quick calculation. "For real, Dad? That's only five weeks off."

"It's real enough. Assuming I don't make anybody mad or break any rules in the meantime. There's still some paperwork…" He paused. "Notification of victims, housing plans, probation details, that sort of thing. There's also one more review before the parole board processes my release. But the doctor wouldn't have told me if he wasn't sure of the outcome. We've been through too much together."

Nate's mind raced. He'd have to make arrangements for Harley to come to L.A. His father would have to find a place to live, a way to earn a living. But all that could wait. "Congratulations," he said. "This is great news."

"It's a lot to take in," Harley said. "To go from having no thoughts about tomorrow to all of a sudden having a future, to having to make decisions. I'm just getting used to the idea."

Nate hadn't had that luxury yet. "Don't worry, Dad. We'll work it out. I'll take care of plans to bring you to Los Angeles, and we'll—"

"No, Nate. I'm not coming to California. That's about all I'm certain of at this moment."

"But where will you go?"

"I'm moving back to Finnegan Cove."

Nate swerved, nearly hit the curb. "What? You can't be serious."

"I'm dead serious."

"But, Dad, you won't be welcomed there. Hell, *I* wouldn't even go back to Finnegan Cove."

"It's the only place I know, Nate," Harley said. "All I've ever known. It's home."

Nate refrained from pointing out that Finnegan Cove hadn't been kind to the Sheltons and chances were, wouldn't be now. "I don't think that's wise."

His father lowered his voice soothingly. "It'll be okay, Nate. I know what I'm doing."

The hell? In the past twenty years maybe a few people had come and gone from the small town on Michigan's western shore, but Nate figured the population would have stayed pretty much the same. Two thousand folks, give or take, lived in comfortable bungalows, and a few fancy Victorian houses from the town's lumber boom days. The same mom-and-pop businesses probably still lined Main Street.

And no doubt the same attitudes prevailed. And memories for certain details had probably only grown sharper. Like Harley Shelton's face on the front page of the *Finnegan Cove Sentinel.* Like the face of his eighteen-year-old son as he'd left the courthouse after the verdict was read. Like the absence of Harley's older son, who hadn't shown up for the trial at all. It baffled Nate why Harley had decided to go back where he wasn't wanted.

"Where will you live, Dad? You think you're going to just put down a welcome mat at your door and neighbors will drop by?"

"No, Nate, I don't. I'm not naive."

"Frankly, I'm beginning to think you are."

"I've found a place to live. A place where nobody'll bother me, and I'll be able to stay pretty much to myself."

"In Finnegan Cove?"

"The outskirts, yes. But I need a little help. It might take a couple of bucks to get this place in shape."

"I don't mind helping you. I've always told you I would, but you've got to be reasonable. Going back to Finnegan Cove is not a good idea. Why don't you consider L.A.? You can start over, make a new life for yourself."

"Believe it or not, son, there are aspects of my old life I remember fondly. It wasn't all bad."

Nate pulled into his underground parking garage, grateful he didn't have to drive anymore. Paying attention to the busy Los Angeles thoroughfare while having this unexpected conversation with his father would tax anybody's ability to concentrate. He parked in his assigned spot. "Where is this place you found, and how did you find it?"

"I read about it in the *Sentinel* about six months ago."

His father read the local newspaper? This man was surprising him more and more. Nate wanted nothing to do with the town, yet his dad maintained his ties. Maybe prison life did that to a person. Made you appreciate what you had before, even if it was less than ideal. "Okay, where is it?" he said.

"It's right on Lake Michigan," Harley told him. "In fact, you know it well." He paused. When Nate didn't say anything, he said, "It's the Cove Lighthouse, Nate. It's for sale."

"The lighthouse?" Nate's voice sounded unnaturally high-pitched in his own ears.

"Yep. It's perfect."

How could a lighthouse be for sale? Weren't they public domain? Nate pictured the wooden structure. Nearly everyone in Finnegan Cove was connected to the lighthouse, some in a good way, some in a bad, and in the case of two families, connected tragically.

But for Nate, the building had been a refuge, one he'd eventually come to think of as his personal space. Almost as if the abandoned structure had needed him as much as he needed it.

Until that night in 1988.

Harley cleared his throat. "Aren't you going to say something?"

Nate tried to keep his voice calm. "The lighthouse is absolutely the worst place you could go. I can't believe you're even considering it."

Harley hesitated. "You have to trust me on this, Nate."

"But it doesn't make sense, Dad."

"I checked into it. The price is right. Eighty thousand dollars."

As if price was the only concern. But Nate followed this thread of thought. "That's all? There can't be much value to the building if that's what they're asking. Who's selling it, anyway?"

"The town council. They've owned it since the Coast Guard deeded it to them in the sixties."

All at once time stood still for Nate. He pictured the six-story beacon tower protruding from the roof of the small cottage flanked by oak trees. He and his father had guided their commercial fishing boat into the channel by its light many times. The closer they got to the lighthouse, the closer they were to home. Those, at least, were good memories, because that was when they'd had a home.

The wheels began to turn in Nate's head as he struggled to come up with a positive aspect to his father's decision. Harley was right about one thing. The Finnegan Cove Lighthouse was remote, sheltered, private. As long as he was set on going back there, maybe this *was* the perfect spot for him.

Nate sat forward, rested his arms on the steering wheel. "Do you know what condition the place is in?" he asked. He wondered when the light station had been built, and seemed to recall a date from the late eighteen hundreds. "It could be falling down."

"I suppose," Harley conceded. "But I saw a picture of it. Doesn't look too bad. And I could fix it up. I'd enjoy doing that."

"We should have somebody look at it, someone who knows about architectural structure," Nate said, hoping this logical step would put an end to his father's irrational plan.

"Fine." He paused. "Maybe I should try to call—"

Sensing what his father was about to say, and knowing how his brother would react to a call from Harley, Nate stopped him. "Let me handle it," he said. He had been gone for two decades, only traveling to Michigan once or twice a year to visit his father at the Foggy Creek Correctional Facility. And he'd never been back to Finnegan Cove. But he did know that Mike, a contractor who lived in Sutter's Point about twenty miles away, was a stranger to both of them now. That was how Mike wanted it. "Let me make the phone call," he said, and then realized, because of his current schedule, there was nothing to keep him in Los Angeles. "Maybe I'll fly out and take a look at the place myself."

"That'd be great, son," his father said, clearly pleased. "I might be seeing you soon, eh?"

"Maybe. I'll talk to you."

He disconnected, shook his head and got out of his car. This was a crazy idea. If that lighthouse hadn't washed into Lake Michigan, it had to be pretty damn close. But all at once the thought of buying that old place, fixing it up…well, maybe his father had hit on an interesting idea. A project like that, both of them working with their hands, as they had in the old days, when they used to pull in nets loaded with the catch of the day, might be exactly what he and Harley needed.

Of course, the first step in evaluating the practicality of this plan wasn't going to be easy. Nate hadn't spoken to his brother in years.

He took the elevator to the fourteenth floor, went inside his condo and got his address book from the desk. He poured himself a gin and tonic and sat at the bar. Then he punched in the phone number of Mike Shelton. Maybe his brother wouldn't be too busy on a Friday evening to talk to him. If he'd talk to him at all.

A kid answered the phone. Nate's nephew. He'd be ten now. "Is Mike there?" Nate asked.

"Yes. Who's calling?"

The boy didn't react to hearing Nate's name, just said he'd get his dad. A few seconds later, his brother came on the line. "Nate?" He didn't even try to hide his surprise. Or the mistrust.

"Yeah, it's me."

"What do you want?"

He pictured his older brother, brawny, muscles bulging from hard work, eyes tired from reading blueprints. The perpetual scowl on his face that Nate hadn't seen in years, but figured was still there. "I have news." Nate waited for a reaction, received none. "Dad's being paroled."

He heard Mike grunt. "They're letting him out?"

"It's been twenty years, Mike. He was due to have a parole hearing."

"Whoopee. And this affects me how?"

Nate thought about suggesting that Mike make an effort to see their father, but he knew the futility of that. Mike lived only two hours away from the peni-tentiary. He'd never once made the trip to Foggy Creek. He'd never even put a stamp on a Christmas card.

"I could use your help," Nate said.

"Hey, if this involves Harley, count me out. You know how I feel."

"Yes, I do, but I'm asking for me."

Nate held his breath, knowing a favor between two estranged brothers wasn't likely to get a more favorable reaction than one between an estranged father and son.

Surprisingly, Mike said, "What do you need me to do?"

"Dad's moving back to Finnegan Cove when he gets out in a few weeks."

"He's what?" The question was a bark of disbe-lief.

"I know. I thought it was a bad idea, too. But he's determined."

"He's a mental case, Nathaniel."

Nate shook his head, not bothering to argue. The Harley Shelton Nate knew today was as calm and rational as anyone he'd ever met. At least that's what Nate had believed until Harley said he was moving back to the Cove.

"Nevertheless," Nate continued, "he's decided to buy the old lighthouse. That's where he wants to live."

"Now I know he's gone off the deep end," Mike said. "Have you seen that place?"

"No. You have?"

"I've been to the Cove a time or two on projects. Drove by it."

"Oh." Nate calmly explained the situation, giving Mike time to criticize between sentences.

"I don't want anything to do with this," Mike said when he'd finished.

"Just look at the place for me," Nate said. "I need a professional opinion on how bad the building is, what it would take to fix it up. Can't you at least meet me down there? You won't have to see Dad."

An uncomfortable silence stretched into long seconds. "All right," Mike finally said. "When are you getting here?"

"I have to take care of some things, but I'll be flying out on Tuesday. Can you meet me in Finnegan Cove on Wednesday morning?"

"I'll meet you at the light station at ten o'clock," Mike said. "Before then, I'll make a couple of calls, see what I can find out about the old place." He paused. "And Nate?"

"Yeah?"

"This is it. Don't ask me to get involved any more than this one visit."

"Okay. Deal."

# CHAPTER TWO

*Finnegan Cove, Michigan*
*April*

JENNA RACED DOWN the narrow coast route. She didn't have to worry about cars approaching on the other side of the road. Few drivers were out at six o'clock on a Wednesday morning. If she hurried, she'd just make it to the bakery in time to help with the first tray of doughnuts.

She stretched her back muscles and stuck her arm out her open window. Maybe staying at the college library until eleven and then grabbing a few hours sleep at a friend's place near campus hadn't been such a good idea. She wasn't exactly the fresh young age of a college kid, who could jump up from an air bed and jog into the start of her day. At thirty-three, she found her muscles were protesting.

She rounded a bend and kept her eyes straight ahead, determined not to look at the lighthouse. But as always, she couldn't resist the haunting pull it had over her. In fact, she slowed her Jeep to a crawl.

The abandoned building rose like a specter in the dawn. Even through the grove of great oak trees, Jenna could see the peeling paint on the tower's exterior walls, the crumbling stairs to the front door of the keeper's cottage. The Fresnel lens at the top of the tower had been removed years before, after some kids had destroyed it with buckshot.

Jenna's grandmother hated to see the building this way. She'd been raised in the small cottage, where her father had been the last light keeper of the Finnegan Cove Station. Hester had fond memories of her childhood along the lake, and the man who'd protected the shoreline. Jenna used to feel the same, but that was before the murder.

The For Sale sign that had been sitting in the yard in front of the lighthouse for over six months creaked in the early morning breeze. To Jenna's knowledge, no one had made an offer or even looked at the place. But that would change if she had her way.

She stepped on the accelerator and sped by. Ten minutes later she swept through the louvered doors that separated the public area of Cove Bakery from the kitchen. Her mother had left the front door unlocked, probably unwise so early in the morning. Everyone, and especially Marion Malloy, knew that crime visited even this normally peaceful town.

Her mother was stacking loaves of fresh-baked bread onto the chrome rack. "Sorry I'm late," Jenna said.

"It's okay. I've got the croissants baking, and three dozen pastries are ready." Marion wiped her hands on her apron. "Have you heard the news?"

News? Jenna had only been gone since yesterday, when she'd left for night class. "Guess not. Something going on?"

"I'll say. Bill Hastings called last night to tell me someone had inquired about buying the lighthouse."

Jenna froze, her hands wrapped around a stainless-steel bowl of dough. "What? Who?"

"I don't know. He didn't say. He just told me that a guy asked the Realtor a lot of questions about the building's condition."

Jenna grabbed a rolling pin and began pushing it furiously over the mound of dough she'd just slapped onto a floured cutting board. "What time is it?"

Marion glanced at her watch. "Twenty minutes after six. Why?"

"I've got somewhere to be at eight-thirty when Shirley gets here."

"Where?"

"Just out."

Marion frowned. "I know what you're doing. You're going to the mayor's office to see what Bill knows about the potential buyer."

*Three Bronx cheers for a mother's radar.* "Maybe I can get him to tell me who's interested."

"Let it go, Jenna. That old building isn't worth your time or worry."

"I know that, Mom. Nobody knows that better than you and me. But I have plans for that place."

Jenna had to strain to hear her what her mother said next, but she thought she could make out "obsession."

"I'm aware of your plans, honey," Marion said, "but I just don't want you drawing attention to our family by pressuring Bill Hastings. People will talk."

Jenna couldn't believe her mother's bland reaction to this possible sale. "I want them to talk, Mom. It will take more money and more people on my side before I can buy that place and tear it down." She stopped rolling out the dough, and stared at her mother. "That lighthouse represents a very sad period of this town's history, not just our own past."

"And how close are you to having a down payment on that eighty thousand?"

Jenna frowned, picked up a cookie cutter and layered perfectly round biscuit dough on a baking sheet. "I just need a few more months, maybe a year."

"I wish you'd forget about this, Jenna," Marion said. "A young woman like you should be looking to the future, thinking about marriage, a family."

"I am thinking about those things. All the time."

Marion sprinkled a row of crullers with cinnamon sugar. "If you're talking about George, then I have to point out that you've been planning this so-called future with him for the past three years, and there's still no ring on your finger."

Jenna gave her a sharp glance. "Do you really want to go there, Mom? Because if we discuss the subject of who's living in the past, I'll point out that you haven't had a date since Daddy died twenty years ago." She immediately regretted she'd said it when she saw the familiar veil of sadness creep over her mother's eyes. Jenna stopped working and reached for her hand. "I'm sorry. That was uncalled for."

Marion shrugged. "Don't apologize. You're right. I just don't want to see you follow the path I've taken. You're only thirty-three. You can still make a life outside of this bakery. You've made a good start by taking nursing classes at the college, but you've got to get over this...*thing* you have about the lighthouse."

Jenna stepped back. "I won't rest until it's torn down and something positive stands in its place. Something that serves Daddy's memory."

Jenna shoved a baking sheet into the oven. "And I *am* making a life, Mom. I'm going to graduate soon. I'll have my nursing degree. And I have George. Once I see a beautiful green park in place of that lighthouse, my life will be just about perfect!"

Marion sighed. Jenna walked by her, picked up a waxed bag and stuffed a half-dozen chocolate-covered doughnuts into it.

"Who are those for?" her mother asked.

"Who else? Bill Hastings." Jenna rattled the bag in the air. "If I can't reach him with gentle persuasion, I know he'll accept a bribe."

"What are you going to do if he does tell you who the interested party is? Are you going to accost the guy?"

Jenna closed the sack and set it aside. "Maybe. Maybe not. Maybe I'll make a friend of him. I'll tell him if he tears down the lighthouse, I'll suggest my plan for something in its place and he can name it the Joseph Malloy—John Doe Park."

TWO HOURS LATER, Jenna entered the reception area of the mayor's office and nodded to Bill Hastings's secretary.

"Morning, Jenna," Lucinda said.

"Hi. Is he in?"

The secretary gave a furtive look over her shoulder. "Well, yeah, I think so. But maybe I should check."

Jenna caught a glimpse of Bill skirting his desk. He'd just grabbed the bottom of the blind on his office door window and started to yank it down when Jenna said, "Never mind. I see him."

She strode into his office. "Hello, Bill."

"Did Marion tell you? I wanted her to break the news, smooth over the situation."

"She told me. No smoothing it over, though."

He raised a hand. "Now, Jenna, don't fly off the handle."

"Who's the buyer, Bill?"

He shook his nearly bald head. "I don't know. The Realtor called to tell me someone was looking at the place. That's all I heard."

"Don't sell it to him. You know I'm planning to buy it."

Bill walked around his desk and squeezed his plump frame between the arms of his chair. "Be reasonable, Jenna. What are you going to do? Have bake sales and car washes to come up with the down payment?"

"I've got a committee behind me. We're slowly getting the money together. We've only had a little over six months. We need more time."

Bill had the decency to look repentant. "I'm not waiting on your committee. But if it makes you feel any better, I didn't think we'd get any other interest. Don't jump to conclusions, however. This is just a first step. The guy will probably back out."

"I don't like the way this whole listing has been handled," Jenna said. "You never called a meeting of citizens to discuss putting the lighthouse up for sale."

"No, but I didn't have to. It's up to my discretion if I feel the entire town needs to be consulted on an issue. And I believed we could handle this decision among council members." He stared at her. "Check the town's policies manual, Jenna."

"The lighthouse belongs to everybody, Bill. You had no right—"

He held up one finger. "Correction. The U.S. Coast Guard sold the station to the town council in 1969. The five council members at the time were listed as co-owners. They were given a legal deed and power of attorney to maintain or sell the property as long as it's in the best interest of the citizens of Finnegan Cove. And each time an election was held and new council members took over, the deed was passed down."

He clasped his hands on top of his desk. "As town leaders, we can decide the future of the light station, Jenna, and that's what we're doing, with the best interest of the town in mind."

She set the bag of doughnuts on his desk and saw his gaze connect with Cove Bakery's trademark steaming cup of coffee. "I've brought doughnuts."

"That was mighty nice of you, Jenna."

"You stop the sale of the lighthouse and I'll bring you a half dozen every morning for the next six months."

He stared longingly at the sack. "As much as I'd like the doughnuts, and you know I'm a big fan of your mama's baking, the matter's out of my hands. The council has voted." He gave her a placating smile. "Besides, all you and your rabble-rousers want to do is tear the place down. The Michigan Beacon Society would be all over my butt if I let you do that. They want every lighthouse in the state saved if possible."

Jenna fumed. He was so missing the point. "It's a decaying old building, Bill. It's unsafe. No one's allowed inside. I want to tear it down and reopen Lighthouse Park. Put in a playground, picnic areas, make it even better than it was before…"

"Jenna, we both know why you want that building

gone," Bill said sympathetically, "and I can understand. I liked Joe."

"Forget about my father. That's my issue, but the Lighthouse Park Committee has a broader goal than just eliminating a tragic eyesore from our shoreline."

Bill shrugged. "Frankly, I don't know why you didn't just set a match to the lighthouse long ago."

"Great idea, Bill. Believe me, I've thought about it. But everyone would know exactly who torched the place, and I'd end up rotting away in prison just like Harley Shelton. The difference is, he deserves what he got!" She snatched up the bag of pastries. "Thanks, but no thanks."

"You're not taking the doughnuts, are you?"

She stared down at the bag. "You didn't give me any information."

"There isn't any to give yet. The potential buyer probably won't even show up. And if he does…"

Lucinda stuck her head in the office. "Excuse me. Bill?"

"What is it, Lucinda?"

"Mark Blayne is on the phone from Sutter's Point Realty." She cast a sideways look at Jenna. "The fella who's interested in the lighthouse is coming to town this morning."

Jenna leaned over the desk. "Won't even show up, huh?"

Lucinda backed up a few steps. "Believe it or not, the original call came from somebody in Sutter's Point."

Bill beamed. "Hot diggety. This guy lives close. He's got to know about the shape that building's in. This is starting out to be a great day." He glanced at Jenna and affected an expression of chagrin. "Sorry, Jenna. But it's the wheels of progress, you know. If there's a chance to get the lighthouse off this town's back, I'm going to take it."

She wanted to strangle him. Instead, she slammed the bag of doughnuts back onto his desk. It made her feel somewhat better to picture his arteries clogged with hundreds of grams of fat. And she decided to find out just exactly who from Sutter's Point was buying the lighthouse out from under her.

JENNA WAS BACK AT THE bakery by nine o'clock, mechanically refilling coffee cups. "Who could this buyer be?" she asked her mother.

Marion gave her a long-suffering look and began arranging clean mugs behind the counter. "He's just looking, Jenna. We don't know that he's going to buy it. So why is it so important that you know his name?"

"Because maybe he's a nice old man who just wants to do something for the community. Maybe I can talk him into donating the lighthouse back to us."

Marion stared at her. "That wouldn't make any sense. No one spends eighty thousand dollars on a lark—at least no one from around here. It's more likely this guy bought it as an investment, and turning it over to you and your committee would be a ridiculous decision."

"Then maybe he's a developer interested in putting something new on that property. He might even like my idea for beautification."

"Jenna, you have to stop concocting these ideas. If you really want to tackle a tough problem, think about what will happen if the place sells and we have to tell your grandmother." Marion sighed. "I'm not sure this town is equipped to handle a rebellion at the seniors home."

"She'll be devastated," Jenna agreed. "But no more than if she discovered my plans for the building."

Marion nodded toward the front window of the shop. "Who's that man across the street? He's just standing there... Maybe he's lost?"

NATE STOPPED on the sidewalk and looked across at the grassy area that separated the two sides of Main Street. New businesses had popped up, but much about Finnegan Cove was familiar. The park benches were freshly painted. The flowers were just beginning to bloom. The brick buildings were solid and clean, their roofs in good repair. It wasn't the sun-washed glitz of Southern California; here there was a sense of reverence for what had come before. For permanence.

Nate didn't want to be here. He hadn't thought about returning to this place since he'd headed his old pickup out of town two weeks after his father's trial and pointed west. Even when he came to Michigan to visit his father, he never considered stopping in Finnegan Cove. There'd been no reason to. Those who'd once befriended the Sheltons had ended up condemning them, along with the ones who'd paid little regard to a struggling fisherman and his two sons.

Before the cancer took her, his mother had had friends. Everyone liked Cheryl Shelton. She'd been sweet and friendly and always offered a helping hand to anyone who needed it. When she died, each of the three Shelton men felt the loss deeply.

Nate looked at his watch. Nine-thirty. He had a half hour before he had to meet Mike at the lighthouse. He headed toward the red-and-white-striped awning over a wooden sign advertising a bakery across the street where there'd once been a dentist's office. He was nervous about seeing Mike again. Even before their mother died, Nate and Mike hadn't seen eye to eye on much. Probably caffeine was the last thing Nate needed before facing his brother, but what the heck.

THE TALL MAN IN JEANS and a light jacket Marion had pointed out was approaching the shop. The sun glinted off his dark-blond hair. His bronzed complexion told Jenna he wasn't from around Finnegan Cove. No one on Lake Michigan had the hint of a tan in April. This guy had to be a transplant from someplace exotic and sunny. Cool and confident—that's what he was, with the emphasis on cool. Residents of Finnegan Cove were solid, dependable, but definitely not cool.

He came inside and looked around. The last customers had left several minutes ago. The sandwich crowd wouldn't be in for lunch for some time.

"Are you open?" the man asked, coming up to the counter.

"Until two," Marion said.

He sat on a bar stool. Something about the man's voice seemed familiar. Jenna studied him closely. He looked familiar, too, as if he was someone she ought to know. But that was impossible. How would she know a guy whose jeans even looked expensive—as if custom-made to fit his long, lean legs? He wore a shirt with a button-down collar. Guys in Finnegan Cove wore Wranglers from Wal-Mart, and T-shirts advertising the local bait-and-tackle hut. She couldn't look away. The stranger was intriguing, and not just because they didn't see many strangers before tourist season.

"I'll have a cup of coffee," he said, and pointed to the chrome cake tray covered with a plastic dome. "And that raspberry Danish."

Marion slid the pastry onto a plate and set it in front of him. She stood a moment, her eyes intent on his face. Then she gasped and covered her mouth with her hand.

Jenna rushed over from the coffee machine. "Mom, are you all right?"

Marion's eyes widened. Her lips twitched, as if

she didn't know whether to smile or frown. "After all these years…"

The man stared hard at her mother, then sat back on the stool. "My God. Marion Malloy?"

She exhaled a long breath and said simply, "Nate."

Jenna dropped the cup she'd been about to fill with coffee. It broke into a dozen pieces. He tore his gaze from Marion's face to look at her, and the past came back in a nightmarish rush. He was Nate Shelton—older, more filled out, without the wiry toughness of youth, and with a few wrinkles around his unforgettable blue eyes.

Marion cleared her throat, hurried to help Jenna clean up the mess. After throwing the shards in the trash can, she broke the awful silence. "You remember my daughter, Jenna, don't you, Nate?"

He gave her an intense appraisal, as if trying to find her in his memory bank. "Sure," he said after several uncomfortable moments. "You were just a kid when I…left."

*You mean when you ran away rather than face what your father had done.* "I was thirteen," she said. "Not so much a kid. Old enough."

"I suppose you're right." He picked up his fork, cut into the pastry and then let it sit there. After a moment he looked at Marion and said, "So have you stayed in Finnegan Cove all this time?"

"I never thought of leaving," she replied. "This is my home. And I bought this shop with the money…" She paused, looked down at the counter. "With the money I got after Joe died. Anyway, this is a nice business. My daughter helps out. We get along just fine."

He nodded, acknowledged the full cup of coffee Jenna placed in front of him. "That's good. I'm happy for you." He took a sip. "You know, I think about what happened a lot. I'm sorry for what you went through."

"Forget it, Nate," Marion said. "It's in the past."

*Forget it?* Jenna rested her hip against the counter and said, "What are you doing here, Nate? I heard you were on the West Coast somewhere. Why have you come back?"

He stared up at her with those blue eyes that used to make her adolescent knees weak. "It's kind of strange, I guess, me being here again. And my reason for being here will seem even stranger."

She waited, raised her eyebrows in question.

"The old lighthouse," he said. "I'm thinking about making an offer on it."

Jenna's heart tripped. She clutched the lapels of her blouse with trembling fingers.

He spoke matter-of-factly, as if his admission wouldn't cut her to her core. "I'm taking a look at it this morning."

"But you don't live in Sutter's Point," she said, her voice harsh and defensive. "The man who's interested in the lighthouse is from Sutter's Point."

"Oh. You must be talking about my brother, Mike. I think he's made some inquiries about the lighthouse in the past few days." Nate gave a half smile. "I see word still travels fast around here."

Jenna closed her eyes. She couldn't look at the handsome face she used to dream about years ago. The face so like his father's.

The son of the man who had killed her dad was planning to buy the lighthouse.

## CHAPTER THREE

NOW THAT HE'D HAD time to really look at Marion, Nate decided she'd hardly aged. Her hair, shorter than he remembered, was still a mass of chestnut-brown curls. Her figure was fuller, but obviously not altered drastically by working in a bakery. And her doe-brown eyes, which he remembered from across a crowded courtroom, still sent regret coursing through him. Almost as much as her daughter's did.

He never would have recognized Jenna. He'd barely paid the slightest attention to the shy young teenager until tragedy had brought them together for a few weeks of judicial agony. She looked nothing like she had as a girl. Jenna Malloy stood at least four inches taller than her mother, with wavy auburn hair to her shoulders. And her eyes, a deep soul-searching green, bored into him with a fierce defiance he couldn't ignore, or blame her for.

In Hollywood, beauty was often measured by degrees of voluptuousness. Jenna was striking because of her prominent cheekbones and straight, slightly upturned nose. He sensed she had an appealing combination of her father's determination and her mother's gentleness.

But it was that defiance he most noticed now. She glared at him and said, "You won't be welcomed back here."

"Jenna!" Marion gasped.

Nate had to consciously stop himself from squirming. He stared directly at Jenna and said, "No problem. I'm not staying."

"Then why are you interested in the lighthouse?"

No evasive tactics from this woman. But Nate was certain this was not the time to bring up his father's future living arrangements. "I have my reasons," he said.

She placed both palms flat on the counter in front of him. "That lighthouse is in terrible shape," she said. "If you're thinking of buying it out of some romantic impulse, you should know it will probably fall down around your feet."

Nate reached for his wallet. "Believe me, romance has nothing to do with this."

Marion wrapped her hand around her daughter's arm. "Jenna, that's enough. Nate has every right to buy the station."

Jenna's eyes clouded. He thought she might be close to tears. "He has *no* rights," she said. "That station is a reminder of one of the worst moments in my life."

Nate pushed the uneaten raspberry Danish and full coffee mug across the counter. "I'm sorry I bothered you," he said, sliding a few bills under his plate. "I didn't know when I came in here that you would be..."

"You thought we would have run years ago, like you did?"

Marion picked up the dishes. "Jenna, please, don't say anything else. Nate doesn't deserve this."

He held up a hand. "It's all right, Mrs. Malloy. I understand where she's coming from." He risked another look at Jenna and discovered her expression had softened, some of the antagonism obviously draining away at her mother's distress. "I would have hoped that the bitterness could have lessened by now," he said to her. "I feel sorry that it hasn't."

He turned away from the counter and headed toward the door. "I have to meet my brother."

Marion came from around the counter and followed him. "How is Mike?" she asked. "I haven't heard anything about him in years."

Nate shrugged. "I don't know much more about him than you probably do," he said. "Mike never contacted us after he left. But I know he's a contractor and he agreed to meet me to evaluate the light station." He glanced at Jenna, whose face was now devoid of emotion. She couldn't care less about Mike or Nate. And he could understand that.

"That's good, anyway," Marion said, as if that detail comforted her.

"Yes, I suppose, but some things never really change."

Nate walked out of the bakery and over to the truck he'd rented. He sat in the driver's seat for several moments before turning on the engine. He still had to face Mike, and this last encounter had left him shaken. He should have thought about the reaction his announcement could have on the Malloys. But he'd been gone for so long.

NATE ARRIVED at the lighthouse five minutes early. He parked his black truck next to the burgundy one with Shelton Contracting Services painted on the driver's door. Mike was doing okay for himself. He was licensed, bonded and considered "no job too big or small." Nate turned off his engine, took a deep breath and got out.

Since Mike was nowhere in sight, Nate leaned against his hood and stared. He'd seen the lighthouse from this angle as often as he had from the lake. The building was as familiar to him as the small two-bedroom cottage his dad had rented on the outskirts of Finnegan Cove, the house where Nate and Mike had grown up. Nate didn't care if he ever saw the house again. He'd believed he'd feel the same way about the light station, but he wasn't so sure now.

When he was young and Lighthouse Park had been meticulously kept, he'd come here on picnics. He came to the woods beside the light when he was a young teenager to do what the older kids did— drink, make out, raise a little hell away from the watchful eyes of parents. And he came to be alone during the difficult period after his mother died, and Mike left, when Harley was becoming the man who would eventually murder someone.

Nate escaped to this very property, ironically—within the hallowed walls of a building originally intended to guide seamen along the coast, and save lives. After Harley was taken away in handcuffs, Nate had never been back. Now, standing in front of the lighthouse that had shaped their lives, looking up at the peeling walls of the tower, he felt only a familiar peace.

A tall, broad-shouldered man came around the side of the building. Nate found himself having to squint to bring the face of his brother into focus. Mike's back was stiff, as if he'd rather be anywhere else on earth. About ten feet away, he ran his hand over his thick hair, which was a few shades darker than Nate's.

Nate pushed off the truck's hood, waiting—for what he didn't know—his hands in his jeans pockets.

Mike crossed his arms over his chest. "How you doing?" he said.

"Good. You been here long?"

"About ten minutes." His brother glanced at the tower. "Guess you can tell she's not in the best of shape."

So they were getting right down to business. "The keeper's cottage doesn't look too horrible," Nate said. "What about the lighthouse itself? How bad is it?"

"It's still standing," Mike stated. "The lock was broken on the back door, so I was able to go inside. At first glance I'd say it's sound. But cosmetically it's pretty much a mess. You won't be able to reach the beacon room without major restoration to the stairs. The entire place needs new windows and doors. The floors are shot. The heating system—forget it. Electrical, well…"

Mike's litany of problems should have discouraged Nate. Oddly, it didn't. He was intrigued. "So how much would it take to make it livable?" he asked.

"Just livable? Without fixing everything that needs attention?"

He nodded. "Dad wants to move in a few weeks from now. He can do a lot of the work himself."

Mike frowned. "Still can't believe it. But anyway, maybe between five and ten grand, if you're not picky and you hire cheap help, or do it yourself." His mouth lifted at the corners, something between a sneer and a grin. Nate couldn't tell. He didn't know this man anymore.

"Did you ever learn how to swing a hammer?" Mike asked.

"I guess you forgot. Dad taught me the same carpentry skills he taught you." Nate extended his left arm, flexed his muscles. No atrophy there. What brawn he had might come from a gym membership, but he was still capable of manual labor.

Mike scuffed the dirt with the toe of his boot.

"Yeah, but I never thought it took with you. You seemed to prefer a pen to a drill."

Nate smiled. "Still do."

"To really modernize, make the place comfortable and restore some charm, you've got to be looking at twenty thousand."

Nate nodded. The project was doable, if their dad wanted to tackle it. "I don't see any Condemned signs."

"No. There's access to all the rooms except the tower. But I'd say the only things living here for a lot of years have been birds and insects."

Friday night, after he'd had time to contemplate his father's phone call, Nate had done an Internet search on the Finnegan Cove, Michigan, lighthouse and been rewarded with a picture of the place. The photo had been taken ten years ago, and even then it was showing signs of significant decay. That had been the point of the photograph. A concerned lighthouse enthusiast had chosen the Finnegan Cove Light to illustrate the desperate need to restore the old buildings.

"So, you think the old man's off his rocker?"

Nate scrubbed his hand over his nape. If he was, then Nate wasn't too far behind him. "I gotta admit," he said, "I couldn't imagine why he'd want to come back here." For some reason, certainly not because he thought his brother was interested, Nate added, "I just had a sample of the way folks feel about us coming back to this town."

"What are you talking about?" Mike asked.

"There's a bakery on Main Street. I stopped there to get a cup of coffee, and you won't believe who's running the place."

Mike waited.

"Marion Malloy and her daughter, Jenna," Nate told him.

"That's an interesting bit of news," Mike said. "I figured rather than relive that night over and over every time they passed the lighthouse those two would get out."

"I know. After I gave Marion the twelve grand, I thought she might start over somewhere else. The trial was hard on both of them, especially Jenna. She was so young to go through something so terrible."

"Getting out is more our style, don't you think?" Mike spat in the dirt, then rubbed his fingers down his jawline. "I have to say, though, dividing up the proceeds from the sale of that fishing boat was the best thing the old man ever did for us."

They remained silent, each lost in his own thoughts, until Mike suddenly said, "So, did you see the daughter?"

"Yeah, she was there this morning."

"She married?"

"I don't know. But I didn't see a ring." He wondered why he'd noticed that detail.

"And I guess she didn't treat you like her favorite person?"

"Person. Creature. Primate." Nate managed a smile. "I'm not high on her list of living beings."

"Was she openly hostile?"

"Oh, yeah. Looking into her eyes, I felt the past twenty years slip away. I was suddenly bad boy Nathaniel Shelton again, only Jenna's contempt was worse than any aimed at me before."

"Hell, Nate, you didn't kill her father."

That simple truth should have put the tragedy in perspective. Sadly, it didn't for Nate.

And he resented his brother's attitude. He always had. Two years older, Mike had taken the brunt of punishment for Harley's erratic behavior after their mom died. It had been Mike who'd bailed Harley out of jail, Mike who'd taken criticism from neighbors and Mike who'd stood up to Harley and argued back when it only pushed the two men further apart. But then Mike left, and at sixteen, Nate had taken over the job of managing the drunken, abusive man his father had become. And Nate couldn't look at his brother today without feeling that Mike had let him down.

Ironically, before the murder, Nate had begun to see a change in their father. Harley had started to resemble the calm, rational, even loving man he used to be. So once Harley went to prison, Nate made strides in reconnecting with him, in time forging a fragile but reassuring bond.

He glanced at Mike, saw him focus on the lighthouse. As in the past, it was impossible to know what was going on in his brother's mind. The only contact Nate had had with Mike over the years was a few notes from his wife, a woman Nate had never met. They'd just shared what Nate told himself was a companionable moment. Could this meeting be the start of a reconnection for them?

Mike turned to him and said, "I haven't got all day, Nate. You want my opinions on this building or not?"

"That's what we're here for," he replied. They started walking toward the lighthouse.

"Just out of curiosity," Mike said. "Did Harley give you a good reason for wanting this place?"

"He gave me a reason. I don't know how good it is. He said Finnegan Cove is the only home he's ever known."

Mike frowned. "Not true. He's spent the past two decades in Foggy Creek."

Nate reminded himself that Mike didn't know Harley was a different man now. "He blended in at prison," Nate said. "I suppose he feels if he can make it there, he can make it in Finnegan Cove again. At least he wants to try. And after spending all those years paying his debt, I guess he's earned the right to live where he wants to."

"Just count me out," Mike said. "I left here twenty-two years ago and I don't intend to come back, even to hang a few new windows. I can't be around the old man."

"You've made that clear," Nate said. "For the past two decades."

"Good. Because I'm doing this for you, little brother. For the years we had together, before it all turned sour." He held up one finger. "No other reason."

They reached the back door and Mike opened it. "I don't imagine he has any competition in trying to buy this place," he said. "If you make an offer, it'll probably be accepted."

"I suppose I will then."

"Then you going back to L.A.?"

"Sure. Once Dad's settled, I'll head back. But as I've done all these years, I'll continue to check how he's getting along." He cut off his words.

Mike's eyes sparked with long-held resentment. "I don't suppose you'd take any advice from me?"

"Not unless it's about fixing up old stairs."

Mike almost smiled. "Okay, then. Let's look her over. You might as well go into this deal with both eyes open."

For the next hour, the brothers examined every inch of the Finnegan Cove light station. And their conversation was all about construction.

In the hours that had passed since Nate's unexpected visit to the bakery, Jenna's anger hadn't abated. Now, at closing time, she feverishly scrubbed the countertop that her mother had just wiped and vented her frustration aloud. "Did you hear what he said, Mom? Nate Shelton feels sorry for me! What does Harley Shelton's son know about anything?

And how does he have the nerve to come back to this town and say that he pities me! How sorry did he feel when his father hit Daddy with that two-by-four?"

Marion looked away, pretending to stuff napkins into an already bulging chrome holder. Jenna saw her cringe. "I did it again, Mom, opened my big mouth. Forgive me. The last thing I want to do is hurt you, and I seem to do it too often by bringing up Daddy's death."

"That's not why I'm upset, Jenna," Marion said. "It's your reaction to Nate this morning. I remember how it was for him. Nate felt terrible about what happened."

"Fine. So Nate felt terrible," Jenna said. "He and his friends were always getting into trouble with the police long before Harley…" Her voice caught, and she took a deep breath. "I'm surprised he didn't end up in a cell before his fifteenth birthday."

Marion stopped fidgeting and looked at her daughter. "I realize Nate did things you never would have done at his age. But he wasn't so bad as a kid. He just grew up too fast. When his mother was alive, he was a sweet boy. And then later, after she died, I seem to remember a few times I caught you staring at him when he was bagging at the supermarket. And I recall picking you up at Lighthouse Park a time or two when you and your girlfriends had gone there to watch the older boys, including Nate, play baseball."

Marion gave one of those knowing smiles that mothers seem to perfect. "You didn't always have such a low opinion of Nate. Besides, the police never charged him with anything. They picked him up twice—and that was only to scare him. Now all of a sudden, he's interested in the lighthouse, and you're dredging up all these reasons why you should hate him."

Jenna had to admit there was some accuracy in her mother's interpretation of history. Five years younger than Nate, and with an overactive imagination, Jenna had often fantasized about him. But after he'd become old enough to drive, Jenna heard more about Nate from the police scanner her father had hooked up in their living room than she did from the few ladies in town he'd managed to fool with his smile.

She knew Nate and his friends hung out at Lighthouse Park, showing little regard for the property, littering the grounds with beer cans and fogging up their car windows with whichever girl in town was eager to take a drive.

Jenna always believed Nate and his friends were the main reason the park got a bad reputation. But even then, while Lighthouse Park deteriorated and the station began its sad decline into disrepair, Marion had defended Nate to Jenna, saying he was just acting out his frustrations. Joseph Malloy, on the other hand, saw Nate for what he was—a bad seed who would end up like his father, quarrelsome, mean, and not to be trusted.

"You know," Marion said now, "you might try being nice to Nate. We don't know what's going to happen with the lighthouse."

She headed into the kitchen and Jenna followed her, saying, "I've been thinking about this all day, and I can't come up with any reason Nate would want to buy the place. But he mentioned Mike, and I'm wondering if he's the one who's interested. Though why Mike would come back is an even greater mystery. He left before Nate did."

Marion organized cans on a shelf. "My daughter the detective," she said fondly.

"Certainly Mike's motive for buying the station can't be better than mine."

"We're finished here," her mom said. She snapped the dead bolt on the back door and turned around. "But one last thing, Jenna. Your motive for wanting to buy the light is as personal and subjective as any could be."

"What? The building is a mess. I want to tear it down and put something beautiful and lasting in its place."

Marion walked over, wrapped her hands around Jenna's arms. "What you really want is to get rid of a horrible memory."

When Jenna started to protest, her mother wouldn't let her. "And I understand." She smoothed her hand over Jenna's shoulder. "I wish you could have been spared what you saw that night. If I could change anything about the past, it would be that, and your grief. The grief you still feel."

Jenna looked at the floor, unable to bear the pain in her mother's expression. They had been through so much, the two of them. Heartache, therapy, starting over. But still, after all this time, Marion didn't really understand.

Her mother leaned down to peer into Jenna's downcast eyes. "It's just a building, honey. Something terrible happened there, but twenty years have passed. You've got to let it go."

"I have, Mom," she protested. "At least I'm trying. I try every day. But the best way, the surest way to put the past to rest is to wipe it off the face of the earth." She hoped her mother could see the sense of what she was saying. "And when that station came up for sale, it was a sign I can't ignore. I was meant to buy that place."

Marion turned and got her purse out of the locker. "You haven't told your grandmother your idea."

"No." That admission plagued Jenna's conscience. She didn't like hiding anything from Hester.

"She'll find out eventually," Marion said. "Are you still going to see her tonight?"

"Yes, but I don't want to argue. I'm bringing her a turkey dinner from the Boston Market. She always likes that."

"Yes, she does."

Jenna watched her mother close up shop and, once outside, get into her dependable Ford and drive away. And then her thoughts turned to Nate. She couldn't help wondering what he had done with his life since leaving Finnegan Cove.

He must have found success on the West Coast.

He apparently had enough money to buy the lighthouse. And he looked, well…good. Very good. Successful, assured, as handsome as she remembered. Yes, physically Nate still lived up to her fantasies. She swallowed. Looks could be deceiving.

## CHAPTER FOUR

AT FIVE O'CLOCK, Jenna headed to Sunshine House with two turkey dinners. She parked and went into the well-kept colonial building where Hester had been living for four years. She saw her grandmother across the lounge.

She must have been to the beauty shop, for her soft silver hair had been clipped and curled. And she'd applied rouge to her cheeks. From the familiar theme song coming from the TV, an episode of *Green Acres* was just ending.

Jenna set her package on a coffee table and went to help Hester with her walker. "Hey, Grandma, how are you tonight?"

Hester turned off the TV. "I'm fine, sweetheart. It's good to see you."

"I got macaroni tonight instead of mashed potatoes. I figured we could use the change."

Hester moved carefully across the wood floor. "Always nice to have change," she said. "Keeps a body young."

Hester seemed deceptively calm, which usually

meant something was up. Jenna set their meal out on the table. "How was your day?"

"Like every other for the most part," Hester said, "which at my age is a good thing." She opened a napkin, placed it on her lap and delicately cleared her throat. "Except for hearing that Nathaniel Shelton is in town."

So that was it. "How'd you find out?" Jenna asked.

"Oh, sweetheart, this is Finnegan Cove. If someone sneezes on one side of town, we say God bless on the other." She stared longingly at the small salt packets on the table. "Wish I could have some of that."

Jenna slid them out of reach. "So, what else did you hear?"

Hester stopped a passing aide. "Susan, would you mind getting me real silverware? I don't like to use the plastic stuff."

"Sure, Hester. Hi, Jenna," the woman said as she went into the dining room.

Jenna opened her bag and pulled out the plastic utensils. "Gran?" Jenna said, "You didn't answer my question."

"Oh, right. Well, the grapevine tells me that Nathaniel is looking to buy our lighthouse." She peered across the table, her eyes as clear as they'd been when Jenna was a child and Hester a young sixty-five. "Is it true?"

"Nate came into the bakery this morning," she replied. "He admitted that he was looking into it."

Hester swallowed a bite of turkey and washed it down with tea. "What for? He lives in California, doesn't he?"

"Yes. He said he has his reasons."

"I knew nothing good would come of this plan to sell the lighthouse. I called Bill myself and told him. The light station should belong to all of us, not the council, and certainly not Nate Shelton."

Jenna chewed slowly, trying to appear thoughtful. "Well, you have to admit, Gran, that the building is in terrible shape. It would cost a small fortune to fix it up. And now it just sits there, abandoned."

Hester pointed her silver fork at Jenna. "You don't give up on something just because it's old or discarded. I remember when people set their watches by its bell, and boats set their courses by its beacon."

"I know, Grandma," Jenna said. She'd once had a similar appreciation for the building. But not anymore. Not since her dad's blood had stained the floors. "But I don't think it's worth saving. It's too far gone. And I'm sorry to say this, but I don't think too many people really care any longer."

"Don't say that to the Michigan Beacon Society," Hester said. "They care about all the lighthouses."

Jenna didn't believe that was true. She couldn't remember anyone from that organization ever visiting the Finnegan Cove Light. But she made a mental note to call the society tomorrow to see if the organization was even aware of their small station.

Hester dabbed her lips with her napkin. "The

building does need a lot of work. I don't know who should take over responsibility for the place, but I can't imagine that it should be Nathaniel Shelton."

Jenna could always count on her grandmother to see the logic of things. "Exactly, Gran. That's just what I think—"

"We need to get to the bottom of this," Hester said. "Send that boy over here to see me."

Jenna dropped her fork. "What? You want to see Nate?"

"Absolutely. I want to know what he's doing here, what his intentions are."

Jenna wasn't sure how she felt about contacting Nate, but she'd always found it impossible to deny her grandmother anything. "If I see him, I'll tell him," she said.

"Not *if*, sweetheart, *when*. I understand if you have reservations about Nate, but get over them. I want to see him."

Jenna sat back and stared at Hester. Her answer was automatic. This was Gran. "Well, okay. *When* I see him, I'll tell him."

BY THE NEXT AFTERNOON Jenna's eyes were tired from intensive research on the Internet. She'd hoped to find a legal precedent that would enable her to challenge the sale of the lighthouse to an individual. Maybe somewhere in the annals of Michigan lighthouse history there was a statute that said decommissioned stations could only be sold to conservancy groups. If that was so, then Jenna's committee might qualify. True, their ultimate goal was not to conserve, but they could get around that detail later by establishing their goals for Lighthouse Park. Unfortunately, her searches had proved futile. In fact, she'd discovered that several of Michigan's one hundred twenty lighthouses were privately owned. Her only hope was that a purchaser must meet some rigid standards.

Just before five o'clock, she placed a call to Lansing. A pleasant-sounding woman answered, "Michigan Beacon Society. We love our lighthouses."

You'd have a hard time loving this one if you were me, Jenna thought. She gave her name and location and explained the reason for her call. "So you see, the Finnegan Cove Lighthouse is now being investigated by a private investor who is seeking to buy it."

"Oh, my, isn't that wonderful?"

Jenna's hope deflated. "Wonderful? Don't you want to know about him, what his intentions are for the light station?"

"Well, yes, ideally," the woman said. "But in fact, it doesn't really matter. Most of these little-known light stations fare much better when they're taken over by private citizens, whether individuals or groups. If this man does any renovation at all, the building will only benefit."

*But I don't want it to benefit. I want it torn down.*

*And I especially don't want it in the hands of a Shelton!*

There was a pause, during which Jenna heard the shuffling of paper. "Where did you say this is?" the woman asked.

"Finnegan Cove on Lake Michigan."

"Let me see if I can find files on that building." After a moment, she said, "Yes, here it is. The Finnegan Cove Light Station located at the juncture of Lake Michigan and Big Bear Channel. Is that right?"

"Yes. The light used to guide barges heading through the channel to Big Bear Lake, where there was a sawmill until the middle of the century."

"It says here that when shipping dried up, an electric navigational device was put in, making the lighthouse unnecessary."

"Well, of course. Once lumber was no longer sent across Lake Michigan, the light was decommissioned. It stood for a while as the focal point of a park, but now even that's gone. No one paid any attention to the lighthouse for years."

"Oh, my, that is sad," the woman said. "At least sixty of our stations are in danger of being destroyed, or are disintegrating on their own."

Especially this one. Jenna figured she was doing the town a favour by tearing down the station rather than watching it slowly and painfully wash into the lake, even if her motives were linked to a personal tragedy. Besides, she wasn't responsible for the property's current condition. If anything, Nate and his friends were by abusing the area for years. And Harley. His actions kept all but the most ghoulish sightseers away.

"We consider private purchase the last chance for some of them," the woman said, "since we don't get nearly what we need from the National Park Service."

"So there's nothing I can do to prevent this private sale?"

The woman seemed astounded at the question. "Why would you want to? Be thankful someone is buying it."

Jenna knew the conversation had come to an end when the woman added, "We simply have too many lighthouses to save them all. But we're doing our best."

"I'm sure you are," Jenna said.

"E-mail us pictures. We love seeing before and after shots. I'm amazed what some people do with our stations."

Jenna disconnected. She rested her chin in her hand and stared out the window of her living room. "You'd be amazed at what happened *in* this light station, too," she said.

Jenna hurried to get ready for her night class. Tomorrow was Friday, her day off from the bakery. She'd have to implement plan B.

"WHAT ARE YOU DOING here?" Shirley asked when Jenna came into the bakery the next morning at eight o'clock.

"I just need to pick something up," she said, smiling at the dozen customers having coffee at the counter as she passed into the kitchen. After surprising her mother with a kiss on the cheek, she helped herself to fresh-from-the-oven raspberry pastries.

"Where are you going with those?" Marion asked.

"Isn't it obvious, Mom? Who, recently returned to this town, likes raspberry Danish?"

Marion watched as she dropped the goodies into a bag. "You're taking those to Nate?"

Jenna smiled. "Absolutely. I can be nice."

Marion pulled a loaf of bread from the oven and poked it, testing its doneness. "I think he'll be as hard to influence as Bill Hastings."

Jenna folded the top of the bag. "Yeah, I remember how well that worked." She headed for the exit. "Wish me luck."

Marion didn't glance up from her baking. "Somehow I think I should be wishing Nate luck. Don't be too hard on him."

Jenna left the bakery and headed two blocks down Main Street before turning onto Sparrow Court. Word had traveled quickly around town that Nate Shelton was back and had taken up temporary residence at Cove Country House, owned by long-time residents Jubal and Bonnie Payne.

Jenna walked three blocks under budding maple and oak trees to the charming three-story home. Like most of the houses on the narrow lanes off Main, it had been built in the early 1900s, at the height of Finnegan Cove's lumber boom. Jenna was thankful she'd been able to buy a carriage house next to one of the Victorians two blocks over on Hummingbird Street.

She opened the gate in the picket fence and proceeded up the brick walkway to the blue-and-white gingerbread house. Jubal greeted her from a rocker on the porch, where he was having coffee and reading the Sutter's Point newspaper. "'Morning, Jenna. Did you come to see Bonnie?" He retreated behind his newspaper. "If you came to see me, I don't know anything about the lighthouse."

"Actually, I've come to see one of your boarders," she said.

The screen door opened and Bonnie Payne stepped onto the porch. Her permed gray hair was meticulous except for three pink plastic curlers still at the top of her head. Jenna wondered if she'd forgotten to pull them out. She wiped her hands on an embroidered apron. "Since I've only got one boarder, I guess it's him you've come to see."

"I expect," Jenna said.

Bonnie fanned her face with the hem of her apron. The scent of maple syrup drifted across the porch. "Whew, that stove is warm this morning. I just made French toast. Nate took his plate to the back garden."

Jubal peeked around his paper. "Where's mine?"

"On the kitchen table. I'm not waiting on you, mister."

"Do you mind if I go around back then?" Jenna asked.

She wondered if Bonnie had even heard the question. She put a finger to her chin and said, "Isn't that something, Nate coming back after all these years?"

"Yes, it's something, all right," Jenna said.

"I know some people spoke ill of him before he left here. He just went through a phase…. But I always thought he was such a charming boy. So industrious." She looked at Jubal. "Remember when he used to come around and clean out the gutters for a couple of bucks?"

Jubal grunted.

"He wanted the money so he could take the bus to Sutter's Point and see a movie on Friday afternoons. He couldn't have been more than twelve."

Jenna pointed to the side of the house. "I'll just go around back—"

"Terrible thing when his mama died," Bonnie continued. "Broke his poor little heart. But he worked until he got his driver's license and his daddy bought him that old truck. I guess he didn't need bus money any longer."

Jenna slowly worked her way to the porch steps. "I'll see if I can find him…"

Bonnie tugged her husband's newspaper to his knees. "What'd Nate say he was doing out in California, Jubal?"

"I think he said he was writing movies." Jubal

stood and headed for the door. "I'm getting my French toast."

"Nate's out back, Jenna," Bonnie repeated. "Why don't you go around and see him?"

Jenna smiled. "I think I will."

She'd almost made it down the steps when the woman added, "I hear Nate's interested in the lighthouse, but I think he'd like a visitor, even if you are put out at him."

Jenna stepped onto the flagstone walk that led around the house.

"You're not going to bring up that ugliness about Harley and your daddy, are you?" Bonnie asked. "We don't want any problems."

"There won't be any," Jenna said. "At least not from me." To avoid another interruption, she strode quickly away. Good grief. Shouldn't Bonnie be warning Nate instead of picking on her?

JENNA STOPPED at the corner of the house and looked over the backyard fence. Nate was there, sitting in a lounge chair in his jeans, his legs stretched out, his leather sandals propped on the edge of a clay planter filled with pansies. Like Jubal, he was reading the paper, but not the one from Sutter's Point. Nate was reading the *Finnegan Cove Sentinel* which had just come out this morning.

Jenna chewed her bottom lip. Now that Nate was close to getting what he wanted, she couldn't imagine why this California man would be interested in the local news and gossip of the town he'd left. Of course, she didn't know why he wanted the lighthouse, either. But in spite of her anger and resentment, looking at Nate Shelton now, relaxing in the spring sun, all she could think about was Bonnie saying that she'd thought of him as "such a charming boy."

Like the confident, swaggering youth Jenna remembered, he still seemed to possess an easy grace that no doubt made him appear comfortable in any environment, fast-paced California or the lazy back garden of Cove Country House. Jenna almost hated to disturb him.

But then a honeybee landed on her arm. She instinctively swatted it with the bag of raspberry Danish, and Nate looked up. "Jenna?"

He got up and came to the back gate and opened it. "Good morning."

"Hi." She handed him the sadly wrinkled bag.

He held it between his thumb and forefinger. "For me?"

"Raspberry Danish. Two of them."

"Thanks. This was nice of you."

"I work at a bakery," she said. "It's no big thing."

He walked back to his lounger, indicating a lawn chair for her. "Somehow, Jenna, I have a hard time thinking of a thoughtful gesture from you as 'no big thing.'"

She sat stiffly. The metal chair was old and rickety. "I deserved that," she said. "I guess the

Danish is a peace offering. I wasn't very welcoming yesterday."

He set the bag on a table next to a syrupy plate that was attracting a variety of flying insects. "Understandable, I suppose."

"I thought maybe we could talk. Start over, sort of."

"Okay."

She saw what looked like a shopping list on the ground, only it wasn't for groceries. Reading upside down, she recognized a few words. *Nails. C-clamps. Putty knife.* "Doing some repairs?" she asked.

He set his newspaper on top of the list. "Thinking along those lines. What do you want to talk about?"

"The lighthouse."

His eyes narrowed. "What about it?"

"Have you bought it? Officially, I mean?"

"I put in an offer."

"A low one?"

"Not very."

She thought of Bill Hastings and his town council cronies' desperation to get rid of the place. "Then you'll probably get it. May I ask what you plan to do with it?"

He stared at her for several seconds. "I'm going to tinker with it for a time, and then consider my options. But ultimately, my decision will be influenced by another person, so…there are variables."

Variables? His answer left her mystified. Was there a Mrs. Nathaniel Shelton? Was she a lighthouse enthusiast? There were a bunch of people like that in the country. The only thing Jenna was certain of was that Nate couldn't be talking about his father. Harley had four more years in Foggy Creek.

A sudden and very creepy thought made her heart pound. It wouldn't hurt to make a phone call to the state corrections bureau to make sure Harley was staying where he belonged. She leveled a stern glare at Nate. "Come on, Nate, why are you buying it?"

"It intrigues me," he said. "I have some time between projects. I thought it might be fun…" He stopped, as if uncertain how to finish.

"Fun? You thought buying the place where your father—" She bit back her words. "You thought returning to Finnegan Cove would be fun? You haven't been here in…"

"Not since the trial."

"That's what I thought. I would have heard."

"I'm sure you would have."

"So why now?"

He paused, stared at the tall hedge at the back of the Paynes' property. "I have my reasons."

Nate was an expert at dodging answers. "Are you going to live in the lighthouse?" she asked.

"Maybe, while I do some renovations. But permanently? No. My home is in California. My work is there."

*And your family, as well?* she wondered. "But what will happen to the light when you've finished *tinkering* as you put it? Will you just leave again? Desert it?"

He picked up a mug and drank from it. Then he studied her for a long, uncomfortable moment. "Maybe I'll sell it, make a profit. I don't know. Like I said, I have a few options."

"But then, why…?"

He set down his mug and leaned toward her. "Look, Jenna, why don't you stop this interrogation and say what's really on your mind? We're obviously no good at reading each other's thoughts. You don't like my answers and I don't have anything else to tell you right now."

She tamped down her rising anger. "I just need to know if the light station will still be here when you leave."

"Why wouldn't it be? It was a part of Finnegan Cove decades before I was born. There's no reason to think it won't survive a few weeks of me living in it." He stood, gathered his dishes, the Danishes, newspaper and writing tablet. "I have errands to run, Jenna, so if there's nothing else…"

He was dismissing her. And all he'd told her was that he intended to tinker, and he had options. Apparently buying the lighthouse was a lark, maybe a trip down memory lane, maybe an attempt to regain something he'd lost. Jenna had to admit the place symbolized a significant loss for several people, including Nate. Could he be buying the station out of some sense of guilt? She stared at him. Confident, relaxed, almost cocky…

Couldn't be.

So maybe he just needed a diversion from whatever it was he did in California. The only clue she had about his life was the hint she'd just gotten from Jubal. If Nathaniel Shelton wrote movie scripts, she should be able to find out on the search engines—if he'd ever made a sale, that is. She carefully got up from the rickety chair. "Thank you for your time."

"No problem. Though I don't know what we accomplished here."

*Oh, yes you do, Nate. Nothing. This conversation couldn't have gone more your way if you had scripted it for one of your so-called movies.* She forced a smile and headed for the gate. "By the way…"

He'd already started for the back door, but stopped and waited. "Yeah?"

"My grandmother wants to see you."

The plate slipped in his hand. Only his quick reflexes saved it from landing on the ground. "Hester? She's still alive?"

"Oh, yes. Ninety and going strong."

"Why does she want to see me?"

"I don't know. But when Hester demands an audience, you'd better go."

He shrugged his shoulders. "I don't know about this, Jenna. Hester always sort of scared me."

She looked down to hide a smile. "I should warn you. She hasn't lost the ability to do that. She lives in Sunshine House at the end of Main Street. You won't need an appointment."

"I guess I'll go over there, then."

"When?"

"This weekend."

"Good thinking. Have a nice day."

## CHAPTER FIVE

NATE SET HIS DISHES on the counter in Mrs. Payne's kitchen. "I'll wash those if you show me where the detergent is," he said.

"Don't be silly. You're a guest here." She rinsed his plate and set it in the drainer. "I see you have a bag from Cove Bakery."

Nate had almost forgotten. He opened it and looked inside. "Raspberry Danish. Kind of squashed."

"Shouldn't matter," Mrs. Payne said. "How nice of Jenna to bring you a welcome-home treat."

Nice, hell. Nate scowled.

Bonnie Payne looped a dish towel over a rod by the window. "How was your visit?"

"It wasn't so much a visit as an inquisition," he said. "There are some bad feelings left over from… Not that I blame Jenna. What my father did changed her life."

"Oh, my, yes. I'm certain she carries around a great deal of resentment still, considering she saw her father's body right after it happened."

Nate cringed.

Unaware of his reaction, Mrs. Payne added, "But I don't think that's why Jenna came here this morning."

"No, I don't either."

"She probably heard you might buy the lighthouse."

*No kidding.* "She seemed to want some sort of assurance from me," Nate said. "A declaration of my intentions."

The woman nodded. "Did you tell her what they are?"

"I'm still not one hundred percent certain my offer is going to be accepted. I'll know later today, though."

Mrs. Payne poured herself a cup of coffee and leaned against the counter. "There's no reason you should listen to me, Nate, but I'm going to give you some advice anyway."

"Okay."

"Jenna Malloy is a good person."

"I'm sure she is."

"She and her grandma are very close. In fact, Jenna's taking nursing courses at the college to be a caregiver of elderly patients."

So far Nate hadn't seen any indication of Jenna's nurturing side, but he was pleased to know she had one.

"And she's good to her mother. Those two work side by side at the bakery. They've always been there for each other…through the tough times."

"That's the impression I got," Nate said, not quite sure what the advice was finally going to be.

"Be nice to Jenna. She's making something of her life, but she's suffered. She needs kindness."

He looked down, smiling. "I'll do my best to be as kind as I can," he said.

"I know you will, honey. I'm sure I wasn't wrong about you all those years ago."

FOR THE FIRST TIME in twenty years, Nate pulled into the parking lot of the Foggy Creek State Correctional Facility without feeling hopeless. He'd just been at the penitentiary in December, but that was before he'd thought his father had any chance of being granted parole.

As he filled out the familiar visitor's paperwork, as he was frisked, scanned and searched for contraband, Nate knew this visit wouldn't be like all the others. The phone call from his father a week ago had guaranteed that.

Nate stood up from the plain metal table in the visiting room when Harley came through the door in his blue denim shirt and chino work pants. His father's coarse gray hair was combed neatly over his ears.

"Hey, Dad," he said. "You look well."

Harley put his hand on Nate's shoulder and left it there for precious moments. "We have a saying in Foggy," he said. "When a fella's parole is about to come up, we say he's on short time. And son, I'm feeling short enough to dangle my feet from the edge of a dime."

"A few weeks, Dad. That's all. And I'll be here to walk out the door with you."

Harley sat in a chair on one side of the table and waited for Nate to sit across from him. They placed their hands on the table in full view of the guard. They knew the proper protocol. They'd faced each other over this same slab of scratched gray metal many times before.

"I still can't get over it—you're staying in Finnegan Cove until they parole me," Harley said.

"I'm not leaving until you're settled. That's what I want to talk to you about."

Harley gave him a tentative grin. "You're not going to try and talk me out of my plans, are you?"

"Would it do me any good?"

"No."

Last night on the phone, they'd argued about Harley's decision to return to the Cove, but Harley had remained adamant.

"Then I guess when I leave here, I'll check that my offer's been accepted and finalize the paperwork," Nate said. "The lighthouse will be ours." He shifted in the hard chair. "I suppose I should tell you something else, too."

Harley's thick gray eyebrows came together in a frown. He was used to bad news and probably figured this was more of it. Maybe it was.

"Mike drove over from Sutter's Point to evaluate the place for me."

Harley jerked back in his chair. "The heck you

say! I didn't think Mike would have anything to do with me ever again. He was an angry young man when he left. My fault, I suppose. I treated him badly."

"Nothing's changed," Nate said. "Mike doesn't want to be involved."

Harley's shoulders sagged. "Now that's more believable." He leaned forward. "How did he seem? Did he talk about his family? How are they?"

Nate had kept his father informed of Mike's life, the limited bit he knew himself. Any attempts Nate had made to connect with his niece and nephew had been rebuffed. Mike had always made it clear he didn't want a relationship with the family he'd left behind, and Mike was a pro at clean breaks. His wife, Wendy, had sent notices when the two kids were born. Nate had responded with a savings bond for each child. And Wendy sent Christmas cards every year with pictures. If Mike knew about this, he didn't say so. At the lighthouse when Nate asked about his family, Mike's answers had been confined to Brian's little league averages and Lauren's dancing accomplishments.

"I guess they're fine," he said now. "Brian's ten and Lauren's eight."

"And Mike's wife? I never met her, but you say she seems nice."

"She does," Nate said. "I've never met her though I've tried a few times." It didn't help that two thousand miles separated the estranged brothers, especially when one of them wouldn't cross the street to share a conversation.

"Is Mike still in construction?"

"Yep. Home renovations mostly. That's why I called and asked him to take a look at the lighthouse."

"I'm surprised he did even that. He must have been shocked when you told him I was moving back to the Cove."

Nate smiled. "That's putting it mildly. He didn't think it was such a good idea."

Harley shook his head. "I'm grateful you've decided to trust me, Nathaniel. Everything's going to be fine."

"So you keep saying."

"And I'll pay you back every dime."

"I know, Dad. I'm not worried about that." Nate cleared his throat. "One thing Mike did mention was the money you split between us when your fishing boat sold. He thought that was a generous gesture." Maybe that was exaggerating, but Nate didn't care. It made Harley smile.

"It was the least I could do for you boys and Marion Malloy. Twelve thousand each wasn't a lot of money, even back then, but if it helped you all start over, I'm glad."

Nate would never forget the image of police officers leading his father out of the courtroom minutes after the expected guilty verdict had been announced. He recalled, too, his dad's face, the silent words he mouthed. *"It'll be okay, son."* Two days later Nate learned that Harley had arranged for his lawyer to settle his affairs. That included selling off his forty-foot trawler.

Harley had arranged a meeting with Nate at the correctional facility and told him to split the proceeds from the sale three ways. "Leave Finnegan Cove, Nate," he'd said. "I know what's in your heart, and you can't pursue it here."

Nate had taken his advice and left for California to enrol in film studies at UCLA. Without that money, his father's gift to him, he didn't know where he'd be today, but he figured he might be looking at the walls of Foggy Creek from a much more personal perspective.

"I saw Marion," he said as an afterthought.

Nate waited for a reaction from his father. He didn't know how Harley would feel about going back once he knew the wife of the man he'd killed was still in town. When his expression didn't change, Nate said, "Dad, Marion Malloy still lives there."

"I've heard."

"And that's all right with you?"

Harley shrugged with an indifference Nate found hard to believe. "I've served my sentence."

"She owns a bakery. Said she set up the business with the money she got after Joe died." Nate figured Harley would make the connection, since the rumors at the time had been that Joe didn't have any insurance.

Harley nodded, looking pleased. "That's good. She deserves some success and happiness."

"Her daughter works there, too," Nate said. "You remember Jenna?"

Harley's eyes misted over and he glanced up at one of the narrow windows at the top of the cement wall. "Poor kid," he said softly. "Hell of a thing to see. Hell of a thing to have to relive in a courtroom." He shook his head. "My biggest regret..." He paused, rubbed his finger down his nose and sniffed.

"I know, Dad. Jenna shouldn't have been there that night. It was...unfortunate."

"I'll never forget her face. She loved her daddy." He blinked hard. "She must hate me."

Nate couldn't sugarcoat the truth, so he changed the subject. "Hey, you want to know more of what Mike said about the station?"

Harley cleared his throat. "Sure do. What have I got to look forward to when I get there?"

Nate chuckled. "A whole lot of work. But I'm moving in on Monday. I can get started on some of the repairs."

"You'd do that?"

"Of course. I've got to keep busy while I'm there waiting for your big day." He shrugged one shoulder. "And between you and me, I don't have much reason to be in California right now." He made a circle on the tabletop with his finger. "I'd have more luck growing corn out of this dust than I have coming up with a winning idea for a script these days." He smiled.

"I'm sure it's only temporary, son," Harley said. "Maybe while you're working at the lighthouse, you'll be inspired."

"Maybe so, Dad."

The guard walked over. "I gave you an extra five minutes, Harley, but time's up."

Nate walked around the table and shook his father's hand. He had a firm grip, and Nate realized for the first time that he found the strength of his father's hand comforting. The two of them had never shown emotion toward each other when Nate was growing up. Not in a good way. Not in a bad.

Even after his wife died, when Harley had stumbled into the house in the middle of the night smelling like the town brewery, Nate had never worried that his father would take his frustration out on him. Mike had been Harley's emotional punching bag until Mike had enough. Harley never laid a hand on Nate. They just had that kind of relationship—distant, cold. Harley had been known to punch the lights out of any other drunk in town who made him mad, but he'd never touched his sons in anger. Or in affection. They had been loners living under the same roof.

Harley slipped his hand from Nate's and did something he'd never done before. He looked at the guard, looked back at Nate, and said, "Doug, would it be okay…"

The guard nodded, and Harley hauled his son close to his chest. The hug left Nate speechless.

"Take care of yourself," Harley said. "And be careful working at that lighthouse. You remember what I taught you about tools."

Nate blinked, brought his father's face into focus. "I'll see you in a few days." Saying that marked another milestone in their lives. It was the first time Nate had ever promised to return soon.

ALL THROUGH THE CHORES Jenna did on her day off, she kept thinking about Nate. His vague answers that morning had angered her, but perhaps even more, had disappointed her. Didn't he realize that his return to Finnegan Cove would inflict pain? Did *he* want to be reminded of what his father had done, of what had to be one of the darkest episodes of his life? She'd never believed Nate was heartless or insensitive, so where was his compassion now?

After putting the last of her groceries away in her pantry, she reached for the telephone. She opened her directory and perused the listings under the heading of Michigan State Government. When she found the number she wanted, she dialed it. A woman's voice droned a greeting. "Michigan Corrections. How can I direct your call?"

"I would like information on a specific inmate at Foggy Creek," Jenna said.

"Are you family?"

"No."

"What is your relationship to the inmate?"

These seemed like standard questions, though Jenna marveled at the privacy a convict obviously received. "I'm a family member of the victim of a crime," she said.

"Hold on."

A few moments later, a man said, "This is Mr. Patterson. What is your name, please?"

Jenna told him.

"Who are you calling about?"

"Harley Shelton." The name tasted bitter on Jenna's tongue.

She heard the tapping of a computer keyboard. "I have the name Malloy on file as a victim contact, but it isn't Jenna."

"You probably have my mother's name, Marion."

"Right. You're the daughter of Joseph Malloy?"

"Yes."

"Okay. How can I help you?"

"I need to know the latest release date you show for Mr. Shelton."

"Hold on. Let me scroll down."

Her heart began to race. Waiting was agony. Thinking about Harley was worse.

"Okay, got it," Mr. Patterson said.

Jenna held her breath.

"Mr. Shelton is due out in June, four years from now."

Jenna blew out a long breath. "So there's been no change in his status?"

"Not that shows here. Anyway, if there had been

a change, your mother would have been notified. It's standard procedure."

A tremendous weight had been lifted from Jenna's shoulders. "Would it be too much trouble to leave you my address? If anything changes with regard to Shelton's release, I'd like to be notified, as well."

"Sure, you can leave it. I'll file it along with your mother's information."

When Jenna hung up, she realized her palms were sweating, and she went into the kitchen to wash her hands. "Okay, that's good," she said aloud, to steady her nerves. "At least you know this much." She looked out her window at the flowers she'd planted two weeks ago. "Now if I could just figure out why Nate wants that light station—!"

Her phone rang again, and she clapped her hand to her chest. She checked the caller ID. *Get a grip, Jenna.*

"Hey, Valerie," she said. Her best friend had grown up in Finnegan Cove, but their friendship had really developed in the past ten years. Valerie was a free spirit, a risk-taker, while Jenna was responsible, careful. They balanced each other, even if Valerie's influence on Jenna was the stronger one. That was fine. Jenna often needed loosening up.

"What'd you find out?" Val asked. "Did Mr. Hollywood sing when you went to see him?"

"He didn't give me anything."

"That settles it. We're going down to Mickey's for

supper. Call George to meet us there when he closes the store. I'll pick you up so you can leave with him later…if that's what you want."

Jenna agreed right away. She needed to be with friends. She needed noise, conversation, real conversation, not cryptic clues that led nowhere. "When can you get here?"

She had showered and dressed and was on the computer when Valerie pulled in the driveway. Jenna had just typed in three words: *Nate Shelton, screenplay.* Before the results appeared, her front door opened and Valerie popped her head inside. "You ready?"

"Yep, but first I have to look something up on the Internet." Her friend had been sympathetic when Jenna told her about Nate's return, although Valerie seemed to remember Nate much as Bonnie Payne did. The difference was that while Bonnie thought of Nate as "charming," Valerie wanted to know if he was still hot. Jenna had grudgingly admitted he was, but that was irrelevant.

Valerie stood behind her now and looked over her shoulder. "Digging up dirt on Nate, I see."

Several pages of listings appeared, indicating over fifty sites including all three search words. When the first one showed a reference to what seemed a prestigious industry award, Jenna gasped.

"Holy crap," Valerie said. "The guy's gotten awards for his screenplays."

Jenna clicked on the link and read aloud, highlighting facts about the screenplay that had garnered Nate the award several years before. She next found a photo of a younger Nate at a Hollywood function delivering his acceptance speech. His sandy-blond hair was elegantly mussed. He wore a casual suit and he was smiling, as he would be when receiving such an honor. And there was an idealism in his expression, as if his life hadn't been blown apart when their fathers met in the lighthouse. And why not? Nate had gotten away. And in sunny California he'd been young, full of promise, handsome…

Valerie sighed. "Oh, my God, I'd forgotten how good-looking he is. Do you see who he looks like?"

Jenna didn't want to confess that she was as fixated on the image as Valerie was. "He doesn't look like anybody," she said. "Just Nate." *Only better, if that's possible.*

"Are you kidding? He looks like a young Robert Redford."

Finding the similarity startling, Jenna quickly navigated back to the search page. She didn't need to be staring at his picture, coming up with adjectives that made her cheeks flush, and brought back high school memories. "I don't see it," she lied.

She clicked on a link to a recent article about him in a film industry magazine and again read aloud. A more mature Nate was being interviewed about "the downside" of his life. He admitted to scripting projects that hadn't succeeded as he'd hoped they would. The reporter, obviously searching for a sensational angle to the piece, asked about his personal life. The perennial bachelor, was he ever lonely?

Jenna paused, pushed her reading glasses to the bridge of her nose. He'd said no, that he was open to getting married but wasn't ready to settle down just yet.

Valerie squeezed Jenna's shoulder. "It's like a two-for-one sale," she said. "He's single *and* gorgeous."

Jenna frowned, shut her computer off and stared at her friend.

"Are you forgetting that he's the son of the man who killed my father, and he's here to destroy my plans for eliminating the physical reminder of that night?"

"The lighthouse?"

"Of course the lighthouse. We're together on this, aren't we, Val? You know I've been saving to buy it since it went up for sale six months ago. We want to see a fitting memorial to my father instead of that decaying building. We certainly don't want Nate to buy it."

Valerie paused, then said, "Truth? You're my friend, and I'd support you no matter what, but I don't care if that building falls down or washes into the lake." Valerie's eyes sparkled, letting Jenna know she was about to say something outrageous. "And are you forgetting what Nate looks like?" she said. "I may never forgive Harley for what he did, but I could forgive Nate if he bought the whole freakin' town."

Jenna grabbed her purse. "Let's go. I'm not wasting any more time."

As she walked to Valerie's car, Jenna wondered if she and Nate actually might have something in common. Apparently neither one of them had found the perfect mate yet. Yes, there was George now. A girl could do a lot worse than George Lockley.

But did the fact that she and Nate were both still single make them unlucky? Unlovable? Were their standards too high? Their self-esteem too low?

No, not Nate. Jenna chewed her bottom lip. And if he wasn't buying the lighthouse for his wife, then who?

## CHAPTER SIX

NATE STOPPED at Sutter's Point Realty on his way back from Foggy Creek. He signed all the necessary papers and arranged to have the cash transferred. The Realtor gave him a key, something rarely done until closing, but Nate figured it was just a formality, since he'd already been using the back entrance. Besides, he assumed the sellers, the town council, didn't think he could do much to destroy the property before it was officially his. Security at the light station obviously hadn't been a priority in the recent past.

Wednesday, when he'd toured the lighthouse with Mike, they'd discovered a few personal items that had fallen into crevices in the building. Plus there had been a portrait on the wall above the fireplace. Nate had read the inscription and a short bio of the man in the photo, Sean O'Hanlon. Nate remembered who he was—the last light keeper at Finnegan Cove Lighthouse, he'd also been Hester MacDonald's father.

When he entered the town boundaries early Friday, Nate swung by the station. He intended to

take down the picture and put it with the other mis-
cellaneous items, which had probably been left by
the long-deceased resident. He'd give them all to
Jenna eventually.

They meant nothing to Nate. When he lived in
Finnegan Cove, he'd never paid attention to the lighthouse's history. He'd appreciated it as a navigational
tool for him and his father when they fished, and he'd
been grateful the building had been there during his
later teen years, when he'd needed to escape. The
lighthouse had played an important role in his life.
More than Jenna Malloy could know. Obviously,
because of her family connections, the light held an
even deeper significance for her.

He parked in front of the keeper's cottage and
used his key to enter by the front door. He took down
the photo, apologizing to old Sean's stern face. Then
he gathered the mementos to take to Jenna. Maybe
she'd be grateful. And maybe the Malloys would
start to think of him as something less than a total
creep. "I'm not, you know," he said to the image of
Sean O'Hanlon leaning against the wall. "I'm just
trying to help my dad."

NATE HAD FILLED A SMALL box. There was no electricity in the lighthouse, so he couldn't stay past
sundown. He carried the carton to his truck and drove
toward Cove Country House. He didn't want to go
there. Dinner would already be over at Bonnie
Payne's dining table, and he hadn't eaten.

As he drove down Main Street he spotted the bakery, closed for the night, with only a soft glow coming from the kitchen. A few doors down, he saw the lights from a bar spilling onto the sidewalk, and heard music. A green neon sign in the window read Mickey's. Nate found a parking spot.

He went into the tavern and, not finding a free table, settled for a stool at the long, polished mahogany bar. He smiled at the waitress, who took his drink order and gave him a menu. As he looked through it he heard a familiar voice, and swiveled the stool to check it out.

Jenna was seated in a booth behind him. She was with four people he didn't recognize, three women and a substantially built guy with a military haircut. The man looked like a marine and he was smiling at Jenna. Nate noticed the guy's hand under the table—on her thigh.

One of the women said something that must have been funny, for everyone laughed. The woman raised her glass and toasted the group. The marine filled all the glasses from a thick pitcher on the table, then returned his hand to Jenna's leg.

Nate felt a twinge in his gut. At first he thought it might be jealousy, but he quickly dismissed that notion. What did he have to be jealous about? Jenna had a boyfriend. So what? She was cute, smart and undeniably sexy in a red V-neck sweater that drew Nate's attention away from the beefy hand resting on her thigh. She was probably nice to everyone in town but him, so of course she'd have a steady guy.

"Hey, you know those people?"

The question made him turn back to the bar. The waitress was tapping her order pad, waiting. "Uh, one of them."

"Why don't you join them? We can bring up an extra chair. Nobody likes to eat alone."

"It's okay," he said. "I prefer it, really." He managed a quick look at the menu and made a selection. Then he took a long swig of his Jack Daniels on the rocks and stared into the glass, not knowing where else to look. If he was in California, and he didn't have a date, he'd be out with friends tonight. They'd probably go to a trendy restaurant and have food that was difficult to pronounce, then end up at a club, where he'd fake a few dance steps. Funny, but listening to the raucous sounds coming from the booth, Nate's typical Friday night didn't seem all that entertaining.

He was into his second Jack Daniels when he heard a woman's loud whisper. Someone, the comedian of the group, he figured, said in a bold, throaty voice, "It's him."

Someone else shushed her, no doubt Jenna.

Nate heard the rustle of clothing, and the next second his shoulder was being tapped by a long pink fingernail. He turned, looking into eyes so blue the color had to come from contact lenses. The woman passed her hand over short, spiky blond hair. "Well, if it isn't Nate Shelton," she said.

He raised his glass slightly. "If it isn't, then I look a lot like him."

"You do indeed." She sat next to him. "You remember me?"

"I ought to," he said.

She held out her hand. "Valerie Devlin. Long-time admirer."

He shook her hand. "Nate Shelton. New admirer." He stole a glance at the booth. Everyone was looking at them. Even Mr. Grab-a-leg had loosened his grip. His clean-shaven chin rested on top of both hands, and his expression almost seemed threatening. Jenna had her eyes trained on her lap, a horrified expression on her face.

Valerie pointed her elegant finger across the aisle. "You see that woman over there, the one who's about to slide under the table?"

Given permission, Nate stared at Jenna. She glanced up, glaring at Valerie. "Sure do," he said.

"She's my best friend." Valerie smiled, a cute, pouty look that would go over well in L.A. "At least she was my friend until now. Will you please tell her what you plan to do with her lighthouse so we can all get back to the business of drinking too much and go home happy?"

Nate took a swallow from his glass. "No. But only because she doesn't like me already, and I don't want to make matters worse."

Valerie leaned close to whisper in his ear. "That's just a facade. Jenna likes everybody. I'll prove it to you."

The waitress brought his meal. Nate looked down

at the plastic basket of something fried. He couldn't remember what he'd ordered.

Valerie stood up, waved to her friends. "Hey, everybody. Don't you want Nate to join us?"

He stole another look over his shoulder. The women smiled and motioned to him—all but Jenna, whose eyes were squeezed shut. Grab-a-leg was scowling. Nate cleared his throat to get the waitress's attention, and pointed to his glass. He was suddenly tempted to get a little smashed. "Oh," Valerie said, affecting a grimace. "That didn't go over as well as I'd hoped."

"It's okay," Nate said. "Every town needs a diplomat. You just need to work on your skills a bit."

She gestured to her pals. "I guess I'll go back now." He raised his eyebrows in a silent agreement and she stepped away. "Sorry for bothering you."

"No problem." He'd been saying that a lot lately.

Nate ate his meal in record time, left too much money on the bar and went outside. He was halfway to his truck when he heard his name called. He stopped and turned. "Jenna?"

She was alone. The night had turned chilly and she had her hands stuffed in the pockets of her jeans. The red sweater stretched tight across her chest. There was a flush on her skin revealed by the V neck. Nate tried not to look as she slowly walked over to him. "That was pretty awful back there," she said.

"No, it's okay."

"Valerie's impulsive, and once she's had a drink or two…"

"She's your friend. She cares. Her tactics are slightly over the top, though."

Jenna took a deep breath. The damn red sweater didn't give with the swell of her breasts, and Nate saw too much flesh. He swallowed. "You and I," she said. "We have some things to work out."

"We do," he agreed.

"But about tonight, just now. That wasn't fair. You were outmanned. I had to come out and tell you so."

"I appreciate that, but I can usually take care of myself."

"I'm sure you can. But I just wanted to say I'm sorry."

"Thanks."

She almost smiled. "Remember that I apologized tonight when you see Gran this weekend. I'm sure you'll think I owe you another apology for that, but you probably won't get it."

"I won't expect it, then."

She rocked forward on the balls of her feet. "This isn't over, you know."

"Oh, I know."

Then she turned and went back to her friends.

# CHAPTER SEVEN

AT EIGHT-THIRTY, George came into the bakery, as he did every Saturday morning. Jenna took a break from handing out doughnuts and coffees-to-go, and poured cups for herself and George. She sat next to him at the end of the counter.

"Are we still on for a movie tonight?" he asked her.

"Sure. What do you want to see?"

"I thought we'd try that new fighter-pilot action movie at the Sutter's Point Cineplex. Is that okay with you? Because if it isn't, I'll be glad to see what you want."

Just like George. Polite. Considerate. Accommodating. So much so that even though Jenna had no interest in seeing a war movie, she didn't have the heart to say so. "That'll be fine, George."

He stirred two helpings of sugar into his coffee and set the spoon on his napkin. When he passed his hand over his close-cropped brown hair, strands sprang back with the same precision that defined everything he did. After ten years in the military,

George was always well groomed, fanatical about health and fitness, and generally set in his ways. Jenna had never heard him raise his voice. Disputes in the hardware store he owned were settled with calm, even-tempered logic. And George always won.

"I forgot to ask how it went with your grandmother on Wednesday," he said, after taking a few sips of coffee.

"About as I thought it would. We talked about Nate's interest in the lighthouse."

"What did she say?"

"She wants to have a private conversation with him."

George frowned. He hadn't officially met Nate yet, but he hadn't said anything good about him last night. Of course, he knew that Jenna and the script-writer were at odds over an important issue.

George hadn't lived in town until he'd inherited his aunt's large home on Main Street three years ago, so he hadn't grown up knowing the Sheltons. But he knew what had sent Harley Shelton to prison, and he sympathized with Jenna's resentment of the two men. "So is he going to see her?"

"Yes. I have to give Nate points for gumption."

"If you ask me, he's got a little too much."

George hardly ever spoke ill of anyone, so Jenna had to take this comment seriously. "Maybe so, but don't be too hard on him," she said. "He might become a customer of yours."

She explained about the shopping list she'd seen

the previous morning. "In this town, you're the only hardware dealer."

George looked at his watch. "So far, I've got no complaints about the guy, Jenna, other than he's giving you a hard time. But if he crosses a line, I'll have a word with him."

Jenna didn't need anyone to fight her battles for her. "That won't be necessary," she told him.

"I've got to open the store in ten minutes," George said. He took a couple of bills from his shirt pocket, which was monogrammed with his name and the name of his store.

Jenna put her hand over his, pressing the bills into his palm. "My treat, George. You have a good day."

He stood and stretched. "You, too. I'll pick you up at six-thirty." He checked his watch again. "Should take us about thirty minutes to get to Sutter's Point. That'll leave us time to grab a burger before the movie."

*Gee, George, I don't know. Maybe you should consider the fact that I eat slower than you.* Jenna wondered what he would do if he ever lost his watch. But he probably had a dozen in a drawer in his house in case of such an emergency. She sighed. George was without a doubt the most dependable man she'd ever dated. She supposed at her age, with her biological clock ticking, she should be thankful for a guy who could provide her with a stable future. And she was. Thankful, that is. Content? Yes, of course. That, too.

She'd almost gotten married once, to a developer who'd come to supervise the construction of high-end condos that went up just north of town. He'd stayed in the area for two years, even taking lesser jobs to be around her. Unfortunately, in the end, it wasn't just their relationship that developed.

A few spy missions with Valerie had enlightened Jenna that the man hadn't been faithful to her, and lied like a slick politician. Jenna's trust had suffered a major blow. Her pride was wounded, too, as well as her common sense. She'd wasted two years on the guy.

Trust wasn't an issue with George. He'd made it clear that he would be happy to sit by a fireplace with Jenna for the rest of his life. He was happy in Finnegan Cove, and while that should have pleased her, it didn't. He'd already done his traveling. She hadn't even begun yet. So though she knew his thoughts were headed toward the altar, Jenna evaded any discussion of the topic. She wasn't ready to commit to George, though she figured someday soon she would be.

She smiled at him as he headed to the exit. He waved and went outside. After she waved back, her smile faded. George stepped aside and glowered at Nate as he passed him on his way into the bakery. Jenna quickly dropped her arm to her side.

Nate came over and looked down at her. "Wasn't that friendly greeting for me?"

"It was a goodbye, not a hello. Now if you want to turn around and walk out…"

He looked out the window and pointed at George, who was crossing the street with a safe six minutes to spare before opening the shop. "I'm assuming, then, that you were waving and smiling at him, not me."

"He's a customer."

"I think he's more than that."

"Right now he's a customer," she repeated.

"He doesn't seem to like me."

"I don't know why you'd think that. Anyway, he owns the hardware store across the street, so if you're going to tinker, you and he are going to have to play nice."

Nate smiled. "I can do that. But no matter how well I play, I doubt you and I will end up head-to-head at the end of the counter like you and he were."

*Not likely at all.* She frowned. "Did you want something, Nate?"

"A raspberry Danish. You've got me hooked."

She headed around the counter and automatically took a sack from the shelf. "You want that to go?"

"No. I've got a few minutes." He straddled a stool. "I'm not really used to being on a clock."

Using tongs, she set a pastry on a plate and slid it across the counter. "How nice for you."

"Do you think I could get a cup of coffee with that?" He looked down at the plate. "And maybe a fork?"

She obliged him. "Anything else?"

"Actually, yes. Since you just used the word *nice*

in a sentence, and since last night we were almost civil to each other for a span of, what? Five minutes?"

She arched her eyebrows, waiting for him to continue.

He sipped his coffee, leaving it black. "It occurred to me that you and I may want the same thing."

She shot him her most skeptical look. "Not unless you're assuming that I like raspberry Danish, which I don't particularly."

"I'm talking about the lighthouse."

"Oh, really? What do *you* want the lighthouse for?"

He smiled, an irritatingly natural, easygoing grin. "I know your family's connection to the station, so don't you and I both want to fix it up?"

Boy. This man didn't have a clue. "And if I do want that?"

"I just think maybe we should work together."

"To what end? I hate to repeat myself, but Nate, why *do* you want to buy the lighthouse?"

"Correction. Why *did* I buy it. I signed the papers yesterday."

She'd known this was going to happen. Even so, hearing Nate announce the purchase with such bland finality sent a wave of regret through her. For now, the symbol of her family's tragedy and her own personal nightmare would stand. "Okay, why *did* you buy it?"

"I told you. I have my reasons."

Great. More getting nowhere. She tried to keep her voice level. "You know, Nate, for a man who supposedly makes his living by putting words in other people's mouths, you say amazingly little yourself."

She realized she'd given him reason to believe that she was interested in him enough to research him.

"Look, Jenna. That station is a part of my past, too. A major chunk of my youth was entwined with that light."

She started to point out that his connection to the light involved partying, drinking and ruining Lighthouse Park. And his father had murdered hers there. The light station stood as a daily heartbreaking reminder. "So you want me to believe you love the light and you simply want to make it better?"

He gave her a half grin. "That perhaps is too simply stated. But yes. I do want to make it better."

After all this time? What a crock.

"And that's where you come in."

A customer from the other end of the counter called to Jenna. She looked over to see him holding his empty coffee cup in the air. "Be right with you, Louie," she said. "Look, Nate, I'm busy here."

"Help me with the renovations."

"What?"

"Listen, I understand you're hurting because of what happened between our fathers…"

Jenna stared down at the countertop.

"Jenna, you know the light better than anyone,

except your grandmother. You know what it was like inside and out. Despite what happened between our...parents, your family is tied to the lighthouse's past. You could help me restore it to its original appearance."

Her stomach quivered. She last thing she wanted to do was become involved with restoring that awful place. She hadn't even been inside it since that night. She shook her head. "No way, Nate. Not interested."

His eyes widened. "Why not?"

The customer called her again and she waved at him impatiently. "Just a minute, Louie." Turning back to Nate, she said, "Why would I want to preserve the place where my father was brutally murdered?"

He took a deep breath. "It's just a building, Jenna. I know it has sad memories for you, but it could be brought back—"

She glared at him. "What part of 'not interested' don't you understand? I don't want to slap a coat of paint over that place. I'm sick of people saying it's 'just a building' when they have no idea what it means to me."

He pursed his lips and remained silent a moment. "Then what do you want to do with it? Why don't you want me to have it?"

She leaned over the counter toward him. "I have my reasons. Now excuse me, I have to get Louie more coffee."

She walked away, thinking how she should be

feeling pretty good about what had just happened. She'd turned down Nate's offer. She'd flung his own words back in his face. So why did she feel as if she was slinking away? And about to cry? She hated that lighthouse. It was a crappy old building with her Dad's blood in its floors.

NATE DROVE THE BLOCK to the hardware store and pulled in front of the metal door bearing a sign that read Lockley Hardware, George Lockley, Owner. Nate didn't get out right away, but sat in his car, thinking. Maybe he should just accept the truth. Jenna hated the sight of him, the memory of him, the very fact that he was a Shelton. They were never going to be friends, so the best he could do right now was to keep his motives to himself.

The face of young Jenna had haunted him over the years. The way she'd appeared when she'd testified against his father, trying valiantly not to cry. But her lips had trembled, her voice kept catching on the words. Her eyes had wandered the room to every place that wasn't filled with his father. She'd tried to find solace in a room filled with tragic reminders.

Jenna had sat in the courthouse next to her mother the day the jury decided Harley's fate. She'd had her hands clasped in her lap, her eyes downcast, until the guilty verdict for second-degree murder was read out. Then she'd looked at Nate. He'd expected to see triumph in her expression, or at least relief. What he hadn't expected was the sadness, as if nothing could make her world right again. The grief in thirteen-year-old Jenna's eyes was one of the reasons he'd left Finnegan Cove.

He'd never quite gotten a handle on his own emotions and, since he hadn't yet been able to justify helping his father when he knew Harley's return would hurt Jenna more, he should just spare himself more guilt and give her a break at the same time. He would simply avoid her. That was what she wanted. But for some reason, that didn't seem so simple. Just like putting emotions on paper wasn't working out for him in his career lately, either.

He reached across the truck seat for his list. If his life this week were one of his screenplays, Nate had no idea how he would end it. Now he had to face Jenna's champion, George Lockley, a man who shouldn't have a grudge against the Sheltons, but apparently did. And Nate couldn't help wondering just what he meant to Jenna.

AN HOUR LATER, Nate put his hardware supplies into the back of his truck, tucked the bill, totaling more than four hundred dollars, into his shirt pocket, and headed down Main Street. George had been civil, the best Nate could have expected, and now he just hoped he'd get the same from Hester MacDonald.

He pulled into the parking lot of Sunshine House and went inside. After inquiring about Jenna's grandmother, he sat in the lobby to wait for her. She appeared a few minutes later, ambling toward him with the aid of a walker. Nate was amazed by how she looked. Gray-haired, sure, but except for a few creases around her eyes and mouth, her skin was smooth. Even before she spoke, he knew by the alertness of her eyes that her mind would be sharp.

He stood when she got close, until she motioned for him to sit back down. She took a chair nearby, then stated, "Nathaniel Shelton."

"One and the same," he said.

"You're still a nice-looking boy."

"And you're still a handsome woman."

She smiled. "Now that we have the pleasantries out of the way, let's talk."

He crossed his legs at his ankles. "You first. I'm here at your invitation."

"All right then. Did you buy the lighthouse?"

"Yes, I did."

"What are you going to do with it?"

"I have a few options…"

"I don't care about your options. I only care about your plans."

"I'm going to fix it up," he said.

"I see." Another resident of Sunshine House buzzed toward them on an electric scooter and slowed when she was within hearing range. Hester waved her off. "I don't listen in on your private conversations, Greta."

The woman huffed, pressed a button on her handlebar and took off.

"You going to live in it?" Hester asked Nate.

"I can't stay in Cove Country House forever."

"Heavens no. Bonnie Payne is a gossip. She'll tell everyone the color of your underwear."

"I don't mind that. It's white. No big deal. It's the no swearing that bothers me."

Hester bit her bottom lip to keep from smiling. "But eventually you're going back to where you came from—California, isn't it?"

"It is, and I am."

"What happens to the lighthouse then?"

Nate had a sudden irrational feeling that lying to Hester MacDonald was almost like lying to God. He didn't know if he could do it. But the longer he kept his father's plans a secret, the better. Nate had felt like a pariah in this town before, and he was on the edge now. He didn't want to be tarred and feathered.

"Someone will be living in it."

Hester remained thoughtful, as if accepting that this was all she was going to get. "Have you given my granddaughter any more specifics than you're giving me?"

"Fewer, actually."

"Then she's not happy."

"Not particularly."

Hester settled back in the armchair. "I love my granddaughter. She's a bit misguided, but I can understand that."

Nate nodded.

"Did you know Jenna was planning to buy the lighthouse?"

He leaned forward, suddenly on alert. "No, I didn't. She never told me that."

"She wants to tear it down."

*"What?"* This was the last thing Nate expected to hear.

"She doesn't know I know that," Hester said. "And I don't want you to tell her I do."

"Okay. But why…?"

"Jenna walked in on…what your father did."

"Yes, that was horrible."

"It was. But no one knows how deeply that affected Jenna."

"I can only imagine."

"No, you can't." Hester leaned forward in turn. "Jenna loved her father, worshipped him. She gave up a lot of her youth to please him, to be the kind of daughter she thought he expected her to be. But when she walked into that lighthouse and saw him lying in a pool of blood, and realized your father had killed him, she stopped, in that instant, being who she was. She'd lost her compass. She didn't know who to be anymore."

Nate had imagined that scene many times. Like everyone else in the courtroom, he'd listened that day as the lawyers had forced Jenna to tell her story. She'd been at home alone with her father that night. He'd seemed agitated enough that he hadn't eaten his dinner. And then he received a phone call from a friend. Joe had hung up and announced that he was going out. When Jenna asked him where, he'd been vague, telling her to stay home, that he'd be back soon.

But she hadn't stayed home. Nate recalled the account she'd given in court about how she'd crept out the back door, gotten into the cargo bed of Joe's truck and hidden under a tarp. She'd waited until the truck stopped, she heard the driver's door slam and her father's footsteps recede before she stuck her head out from under the cover to see where they were—the lighthouse.

She'd heard shouting. And then silence. She jumped out from the truck bed and ran toward the building. She met someone coming from around the side. And she recognized him as Harley Shelton. She said Harley tried to stop her from going inside, but she'd found her father on the floor there, a bloody two-by-four next to his body.

Nate shivered, and shifted in the chair. "I remember Jenna's recounting of the events very well," he said uncomfortably.

"Then you remember that she couldn't recall what happened after she saw her father's body?"

"Yes."

"It was your dad who flagged down a passing car and told the driver to call the police. And an ambulance, though he already knew Joseph was dead. I think he called the ambulance for Jenna."

Nate nodded. Harley had told him that Jenna had been unconsolable.

"Your father might have gotten away with murder,"

Hester said. "A good defense lawyer could have discredited the testimony of a distraught teen. But from the first, Harley admitted his guilt."

"I know."

"Why did he do that, Nate? Why didn't he try to avoid jail?"

Nate shook his head. He'd asked himself that question many times. And he'd come up with the only answer he could live with, the only one that made sense. "I suppose because he was guilty," he said.

Hester sighed. "Yes, he was."

"Surely you didn't call me here to go over the details of the trial."

"No. I wanted to talk to you about saving the lighthouse. It's in terrible condition, you know."

"But your granddaughter—"

"Doesn't know what she wants. She thinks all the memories will go away if the building disappears. You and I both know that's foolish."

Nate didn't know how to respond.

"You fix that place up, Nate. Make it shine, for whatever reason you have. Let's not tear down something that meant so much to so many people."

He narrowed his eyes. This was not what he'd expected when he came here. To be in collusion with Hester MacDonald to save the lighthouse? He didn't know if he liked that scenario.

"You make her see, Nate," Hester said. "You're smart. Help Jenna see that we have to learn to live with the past, the best we can. We don't destroy it because it won't go quietly." She reached over and patted his hand. "You understand?"

"I understand, but Jenna is strong-willed. I don't know what I can do."

"I trust you to come up with a plan. And, Nate, don't mess this up."

## CHAPTER EIGHT

THE NEXT MORNING at ten o'clock—her one day off—Marion put the finishing touches on her makeup, smoothed any wrinkles from her skirt and called her best friend, Beatrice. "It's Sunday, Bea," she said. "I'm going today. You know the drill."

"What did you tell Jenna this time?" she asked.

"I said we were playing Scrabble and you were fixing lunch. So if she calls looking for me…"

"I know. You're in the bathroom. You just left to go to the grocery store. You decided to get a jump on Monday and you're at the shop baking bread—"

"No! Don't tell her that. She'll show up to help me."

Bea laughed. "I'm kidding, Marion. It's not like I just started lying for you yesterday. Don't worry. I'll make it convincing."

Marion's breathing returned to normal. "I know you will, honey. Have I ever told you how much I appreciate what you do for me?"

"Yes, many times, but it's still nice to hear."

"You're the only one I would trust with this."

"To my grave, girlfriend. That's where this secret is going, unless you tell it first."

"Funny, but since Nate came to town, I have a feeling that it's going to come out even sooner than I'd planned."

"You knew this would happen eventually. I'm in your corner, you know that, Marion, but you've been playing a dangerous game."

"I suppose. But I just never saw an easy way out."

"Maybe that's because there isn't one," Bea said. "Anyway, enjoy the day. I'll talk to you later."

Marion hung up the phone, went out her front door and got into her car. She took a moment to appreciate the perfect weather for a drive and then picked up a bakery menu from the passenger seat and fanned her face. These Sunday excursions always seemed to activate some internal furnace.

An hour and fifteen minutes later she pulled into the parking lot of the Foggy Creek Correctional Facility. The guard who checked her for contraband knew her. He'd worked at the penitentiary for years. He spoke to her as an old friend, patted her down quickly and released the gate that led to the main visitors' lounge. She took a seat at a table for two in the corner, laced her hands in her lap and waited.

Harley entered a few minutes later. A wide smile lit his face when he saw her, and he strode across the room. Taking her hands, he pulled her to her feet and enclosed her in his strong arms. And then he kissed her, not on the cheek like he usually did when the guards turned their heads, but full on the mouth.

She pushed at his chest. "Harley, you'll get in trouble for sure if the guard sees us."

He chuckled deep in his throat. "Look over there, honey. Do you see a frown on O'Toole's face?"

She peeked around Harley. The muscular guard grinned and raised his hand from his holstered weapon to give her a wave.

"I told him when I got to the door that I was going to flat-out kiss you today."

"What did he say?"

"He said, 'Go for it. You're a short-timer anyway.'"

Marion looked over at the guard once more and raised her eyebrows in an unspoken question. O'Toole surveyed the room carefully, as if to note that they were the only people present before the official noon visiting hour. Then he shrugged. So Marion kissed Harley this time. "It's nice to be able to do that," she said.

"You bet it is, though not as nice as that extended visit last month."

Marion blushed as she sat down. "Only a few weeks, honey."

Harley sat opposite her. "I'm marking the days."

She squeezed his hand. "It's going to be so good having you in Finnegan Cove."

He rubbed a finger over his chin. "But there will

be problems. And we can't avoid talking about them any longer."

She sighed. "Jenna." The single word settled like a dark cloud over the drab room that had been their meeting place for twenty years.

Harley shook his head. A lock of thick gray hair fell onto his forehead. He ignored it, but Marion brushed it back.

"You should have told her about us, love," he said. She started to protest, but he held up his hand. "All these years of you coming here. It's just not right. It makes what I feel for you seem cheap and deceitful. And that's the last thing I want."

"I know that, Harley. But you've always agreed that I could handle this my way. There's never been a right time to tell her. I'd start to, and then she'd say something about her daddy and I'd lose my nerve. It just seemed that Jenna held on to the anger for so long that confessing the truth to her would have broken what faith she had in me."

"It's only going to be more difficult now," Harley said. "Are you going to tell her the whole story before I get out?"

"I don't know. Certain things she'll have to know. But it will be hard to tell her about her father. Joe and I always kept up a good image for Jenna. I'll decide when the time comes."

Harley smiled. "Marion, it's coming. The clock's ticking."

She reached up and pressed her palm against his

cheek. "It'll be all right. Trust me, Harley. Jenna may surprise us both with her capacity to forgive."

His expression turned serious. "Marion, when you feel the time is right, let me tell her what happened. It might make a difference. Or at least let's tell her together."

"You know, Harley, that could be a good idea. Once Jenna understands our commitment to each other, she might be more willing to listen."

"What happened in the past isn't the only problem, Marion. You know that. Jenna won't be happy with me living so close to town, in the lighthouse."

Marion dropped her hands to her lap and squeezed them together tightly. She'd been over this so many times in her head, and she'd always came to the same conclusion. She'd sacrificed a lot over the years. She deserved some happiness now, while it was within her grasp. Even Jenna had told her that.

Marion hadn't told Harley that her daughter wanted to tear down the lighthouse, and she didn't tell him now. "I want us to have it," she said. She reached over and clasped Harley's hand. "My happiest days were in that lighthouse. I intend to have many more there, too."

Harley smiled. "If you feel that strongly, then we're doing the right thing."

She squeezed his hand. "Jenna will forgive us. You'll see. She'll be disappointed at first, but in time she'll put her energy into another project, one that isn't all knotted up with the past. And she'll move forward once she realizes that the lighthouse can still be beautiful."

"Maybe that station going up for sale was a sign, Marion, coming right before my parole. Maybe we can make this work for all of us."

"I'm sure we can, honey." Marion wanted to believe that, but feared that her happiness might come with a great cost.

JENNA GOT HOME from her evening class a little after nine o'clock Tuesday night. She pulled into her drive, gathered her textbooks and headed to the front door. The street was quiet as usual at this time of night. The glow from the streetlamps and her porch light lit her way up the sidewalk. She'd just put her key in the lock when a truck pulled in behind her Jeep. She instantly knew who it was. George, who rarely showed up without calling first, drove a tan truck. This one was black.

Nate got out, walked toward her and stood on the porch. He had a box under his arm. "Hey. How's everything?" he said.

She withdrew her key from the door. "Okay. What are you doing here?"

"I moved out of Cove Country House. I thought you might like to know my new address."

"I thought you had a California address."

"Well, yes. This one's only temporary. It's the lighthouse."

"Congratulations. It must feel wonderful to be a second-home owner."

"It's okay, but as you know, my new digs need a lot of work. I cleaned the place up pretty well on Sunday and Monday, got the electricity and gas reconnected, but that was just a start. I also went into Sutter's Point to a furniture store. I have a bed, a sofa, a TV. I get four channels with the rabbit ears." He smiled. "I guess your great-grandfather never thought to install cable or at least put up a satellite dish."

She narrowed her eyes. Why was Nate being so charming? He'd just told her he'd moved into the worst possible place. Maybe charm was his way of rubbing her nose in his success. "Why aren't you at home watching one of those channels now?" she said. "I'll bet there's something really good on."

"Oh, I'm anxious to get back and check it out. Can't wait to watch celebrities dance or people throw other people off islands." He grinned again. "Actually, that last show reminds me a lot of Finnegan Cove."

She turned toward her door and unlocked it. "No one has thrown you out yet, Nate. But some of us are thinking about it." She opened the door, flipped on the light switch. "Well, if there's nothing else, I'll be seeing you around." She stepped inside and set her purse and books on the entry table. "I've got a lot to do, now that I have to go through all my catalogs looking for your housewarming gift."

Jenna started to close the door, but he stuck the toe of his boot inside. "Can I come in?"

She glared at him. "No."

"Aren't you the least bit curious about what I have in the box?"

She *had* been curious. And now that he'd mentioned it, she found herself extraordinarily so.

"What's in here is for you," he added.

"Thanks." She held out her hands. "Just give me the box."

He clasped it close to his chest. "I can't do that. Fanfare is needed."

A bark of laughter escaped her. "Fanfare?"

"That's right." He stared down into the box and pretended that whatever was in there was absolutely fascinating. "Just invite me in, serve up a tall, cool glass of water, and I'll show you everything."

She put her hands on her hips. "I'm not sure what's in there is worth the price of a glass of water."

Nate could sense her relenting. He tapped the side of the box with his fingertip. "It's worth it."

She held the door open and stepped aside, and Nate walked into her living room.

He'd expected her place to be furnished with solid, practical items. Boy, was he wrong. Tiny roses climbed the wallpaper to the crown molding around her ceilings. A delicate green-sprigged print covered her cushy sofa. Antique portraits adorned her mantel along with a pair of cast-iron candlesticks. Pastoral prints hung on her walls. "Nice," he said.

"Thanks." She stood with her arms across her chest. "How long will this take?"

"Minutes at least."

"Okay. Then you can sit." She indicated a bamboo chair with a plush cushion. It barely looked substantial enough to hold his weight, but he sat—carefully.

"How did it go with Gran?" Jenna asked.

He shrugged. "You know how it is with old friends."

"That bad, huh?"

"I've had worse encounters with the women in your family."

"Oh, really? I'm sorry to hear that." She smiled slightly. Not a real grin, more an acknowledgment. "So what did you promise her?"

"Anything, to get out of there alive."

"I'll get your water." She came back from the kitchen a minute later and handed him a cold bottle.

He looked at the grocery store label. "Wow, the pricey stuff."

She sat on the sofa. "So what's in the box?"

He took the first item from the carton. "My brother and I gave the lighthouse a thorough examination the other day. We found some things that have obviously been there for years." He handed her an old shaving mug.

She cradled it in one hand while examining the brush, its bristles stiff with age. Holding it up to her nose, she sniffed. "Pine."

"Incredible, isn't it?" Nate said. "I could smell it

too, and the thing's got to be over fifty years old. Nobody uses shaving gear like that anymore."

"Where did you find it?"

"Behind the pipes under the sink in the bathroom."

She sucked in a trembling breath. The mood had suddenly changed. "Wow, this had to belong to…"

He reached out and turned the mug so she could see the back. "Look. The initials. S.O."

She nodded. "My great-grandfather…"

Nate reached back in the box for an old waxed bag and held it out to her. "From the shelf in the bedroom closet, tucked in a corner. I wasn't tall enough to see it, but Mike found it when he ran his hand along the wood."

She set down the mug and opened the sack, letting the contents spill into her hand. "Brass buttons." She examined them closely. "They all have the Coast Guard insignia." Thoughtfully, she ran her thumb over the textured surface of one.

Nate took the next-to-last item from the box, a sheaf of envelopes and postcards tied with a tattered blue ribbon. "This was in the closet, too."

Jenna pulled an envelope from the stack and opened it. She read silently. When she looked up at Nate, her eyes had misted over. "This is from someone who stopped at the lighthouse in…" She consulted the date. "It looks like 1939. Roland Marquart. He stayed one night when it was storming. This letter is thanking my great-grandfather for taking him in."

She folded the letter and returned it to the envelope. "Did you read these?" she asked.

He thought briefly about lying, but opted for the truth. He'd spent an hour last night poring over every missive. "Yeah. It's neat stuff. Your great-grandfather was well liked."

She thumbed through the letters gently. "I never knew him. He died in 1962, when my mother was ten. She remembers him."

"Is that when the Coast Guard decommissioned the light?"

"No. They ordered it shut down for good in 1960. Gran had moved back in eight years earlier, when her husband was killed in Korea. The town council let her stay there with my mom until 1965, when they both moved out. Gran couldn't keep it up by herself."

Tucked in the back of Nate's mind was the news he'd gotten from Hester on Saturday. Looking at Jenna now, he saw a sadness in her eyes. It was a damn shame that her father's death had destroyed her connection to the lighthouse—to the point that Jenna only wanted to tear it down.

He wished he could fix that for her.

She wiped her eyes and leaned over the box. "Is there anything else?"

"A brochure." He took it out and passed it to her.

She turned it over in her hand. When she looked at him, her expression reflected her confusion. "These are paint samples from the hardware store."

"I know. George gave them to me."

"But why are you showing me?"

"I don't know what color to paint a lighthouse, Jenna. Neither does George. He told me he's only been in Michigan three years. And I don't think he really cares so much about old light stations."

She held the brochure out. "Nate, I told you. I can't—"

He covered her hand with his. "Jenna, I'm not asking you to pick up a paintbrush. I'll do the work. I want to do it. But I don't want to mess this up. Just tell me what color to choose."

For some reason her reaction meant more to him than any he'd ever gotten from a studio head. He gently squeezed her fingers. "Please."

She pulled her hand away, exhaled a long breath and slowly opened the brochure. After a few moments she pointed to a color pallette. "These three hues are perfect," she said. "All smaller stations like ours were white, most with black trim on the beacon tower, so the paler color would stand out more clearly to sailors. And just a hint of this brick-red, perhaps around the windows."

He took the brochure, folded it and put it in his shirt pocket. "Thank you, Jenna." After he stood, he reached for her hand again to help her rise. She hesitated, then let him. That's what gave him the courage to say, "If you want to come by, I'll be working most of the time. It'd be okay."

Her bottom lip quivered. "I couldn't…."

"Okay. I understand." He should go, he knew. "Oh, there's a portrait in the parlor."

"The one of Sean?"

"Yes. Your family should have it."

"No, the lighthouse should have it. It belongs there. You can do what you please with it, but if you left it over the fireplace, that would be okay."

He still held her hand as they stood there. Jenna drew in a trembling breath, then blinked. When Nate reached up and stroked his finger down her cheek, she jerked back, and his hand slipped to her shoulder. More than anything he wanted to kiss her, to take away her grief. But he was a Shelton, and the Sheltons had put it there. Still, her full lips drew him toward her.

As if she sensed what he was thinking, she took two steps away from him. "You'd better go."

"I suppose."

"Thanks for bringing these things."

"You're welcome." He picked up the empty box and went out the door.

Jenna shut it and leaned against it, her heart racing. Something had almost happened a moment ago. Something she wasn't prepared for. Something she didn't want and couldn't handle.

Nate was the entirely wrong person to make her feel this way.

## CHAPTER NINE

THREE DAYS LATER, Nate had made significant progress in returning the lighthouse to a livable condition. It was a good thing. May had arrived, and Harley would be here in three weeks.

Nate had sanded and painted the cupboards and floors in the kitchen, bedroom and parlor. New appliances had been delivered. A plumber had checked out the well system and replaced the old pipes in the kitchen and bathroom. Nate had picked up gallons of paint from George and was planning to start sanding the outside tomorrow.

But today he turned his attention to the beacon tower, which was reached through a door in the kitchen. Gingerly, he tried the first few steps in a series of stairs that zigzagged upward for six stories. They creaked, and one bent in the middle. Not a good sign.

"Hey, anybody in here?"

The shout brought him back to ground level. The voice was familiar and unexpected. Nate stepped back into the kitchen and saw Mike inspecting his work on the cupboard doors.

His brother lightly tapped the new finish. "Dry. And a nice job, little brother." His gaze roamed over every cabinet. "Couldn't you have been more original? Everything's white."

Nate suppressed a grin. "There was a sale on white."

"There always is," Mike said, glancing down. "The floor looks decent."

"Only 'decent'? I used an electric sander. Took me four hours to prepare the floors in three rooms before I stained them all."

Mike looked at Nate's hands, still spotted with telltale color. "I can tell. Didn't you wear gloves?"

"You always told me gloves were for sissies."

Mike turned the new spigot on the sink. Water gushed out in a steady stream. "You didn't do this."

"Nope. Only a fool hires himself as a plumber."

Mike glanced up at the kitchen ceiling, where water stains still showed where the roof had leaked. "Right. And there certainly are no fools involved in this project."

"I don't remember inviting you to this housewarming, Mike."

"You didn't. And believe me, I didn't drive here from Sutter's Point just to see what you've done."

"Then why are you here?"

"Had a couple of projects in the area to bid on. Figured as long as I was in the neighborhood I should at least see if you've sawed off a finger or driven a nail through your thumb."

Nate examined his hand. "Sorry to disappoint you."

Mike nodded at the new three-piece dining set in the middle of the kitchen. "You gonna offer me a seat?"

Nate opened the refrigerator and took out a bottle. "And a beer if you want one."

"I don't drink much anymore, but for you I'll make an exception." He sat down, twisted off the cap with ease and took a long pull. "So how's everyone treating you?"

Nate got a beer for himself and joined him at the table. "There's a waitress at Mickey's who's not bad to me. And this woman, Valerie. She's actually kind of friendly."

Mike's eyes registered instant recognition. He held the bottle suspended halfway to his mouth. "Valerie Devlin? Three years younger than me?"

"Could be."

"You didn't remember her?"

"Only vaguely. But it's obvious your memory is quite specific."

"Damn. She's still here. She was so out of our league."

Nate took a swallow. "I think she could be a player now."

"Figures. When I'm not in the game anymore." He lifted his beer to his lips. "What about Jenna Malloy? She still busting your balls?"

Nate smiled, as he had frequently over the last few

days, whenever he thought of Jenna. "She's trying to, but I think she's finding it more difficult."

"You're winning her over?"

"I wouldn't go that far. But the next time I see her, I won't be looking for any concealed weapons."

His brother shook his head. "I have to give you credit. You're sticking it out in this town. I wouldn't do it."

"It's not so bad."

Mike upended his bottle and finished off the beer in a couple of long gulps. "What were you doing when I got here? You were in the tower, right?"

"Yeah. I'm anxious to go up. I remember the view from when I was a kid. The stairs aren't in the best shape, though. I was just about to start fixing them."

"You got extra lumber?"

"Inside the door, leaning against the wall."

"You make me a sandwich, I'll have a look at 'em."

"It's a deal."

Three hours later, Mike had downed two sandwiches and two more beers. And he'd gotten as far as the fourth story. "I have to quit," he said when he came down. "I'm not saying those stairs are perfect—many of them should be replaced. But you can go up them if you don't stomp around too much. Did you watch what I did? How I firmed up the supports?"

"I did. I know what to do. In fact, I was thinking—if I need advice on painting the outside, maybe you'd—"

"Hold on. You don't need painting instructions."

"No. But I was thinking about that book, Tom Sawyer—"

"Forget it. Besides I'm not coming back." He pivoted slowly, giving the kitchen a thorough scrutiny. "This is the one and only time I'll ever see this place again."

"Sure. I understand."

He picked up his ball cap, which had the name of his company embroidered across the top, then stopped at the back door. "Look, Nate…"

"Yeah?"

Mike handed Nate a business card. "You got my home phone number. This has my cell. I just thought that if you're ever in my territory, you could give me a call. I get that you resented my leaving back then, but my past with Dad wasn't like yours."

"I know. Dad was harder on you than he was on me. I guess he thought you could take it."

"Well, I couldn't. And frankly, you sticking up for him then felt like you abandoned me in a way, too. I had to make a break from both of you. And then the years passed…"

"Right." Nate swallowed the bitter taste in his mouth with a gulp of beer and tapped the business card. "So why are you giving me this now?"

"Maybe you could stop by the house or something."

Nate took the card. "Maybe I could."

"Don't even think of bringing the old man."

"No, I wouldn't."

He settled the cap low over his brow. "Okay then."

"Okay. Thanks, Mike. I appreciate you helping me today."

Mike gave him a brief salute and left. And Nate grinned as if it was Christmas morning and he still believed in Santa Claus.

WHEN SHE HEARD A CAR in her driveway, Jenna closed her textbook on Community Nursing Care Management and went to the window. Who could be coming to see her on a Friday near dinnertime? Everyone knew she caught up on her studies on her day off. She quickly examined her scruffy clothes—sweatpants and a T-shirt—and was relieved to see her mother get out of her car. When Marion came inside, Jenna said, "Hi, Mom. What's up?"

"I thought you might want to go out and grab a bite to eat. Do you have plans?"

"Not till later. I'm going out with George, but I'm planning to study for a while longer."

"That's okay. We'll do it another time."

Jenna thought that would be the end of the conversation, but Marion walked into the living room and settled herself on the sofa.

"Is there something else?" Jenna asked her.

"I was just wondering if you've seen Nate since he brought you those things from the lighthouse."

Jenna had shown her mother the mementos, and

Marion had seemed as touched by the items as Jenna was. They'd talked for quite a while about what life must have been like for Sean O'Hanlon and his young daughter, living in the station in the first half of the last century. Marion recalled her years at the lighthouse, as well. Jenna had been surprised that her mother seemed to have such an attachment to the place. She'd moved out when she was only thirteen.

"No, I haven't seen him," Jenna said. "I've been busy. Classes, studying, working…"

Marion smiled. "I know what all you do, honey."

Jenna sat in her overstuffed armchair. "Even if I wasn't busy, I wouldn't try to see Nate. Why would I?"

"I don't know. To thank him, maybe."

"I did thank him."

"Oh. I hear he's been working really hard at the station. I'll bet it's showing some improvement by now."

Jenna remained silent. This discussion had to be leading somewhere.

Marion fidgeted with the hem of her shorts. "Aren't you wondering what he's done over there?"

"Unless he's tearing it down board by board, I don't care."

"I just thought that after he brought you those things, after you and I talked, that maybe…"

"Maybe what, Mom?"

Marion leaned forward. "That maybe you'd had a change of heart. That you'd accepted that the building wouldn't be destroyed."

"There's not a whole lot I can do about it."

"Why don't you take a drive out there? I know Nate would appreciate the company. He's working alone all day…"

"Mom, what are you getting at? You sound as if you trust Nate Shelton all of a sudden. As if he's this savior who's come to resurrect our past. Have you forgotten there's very little about our past I want to see a Shelton resurrect?"

Marion scowled. "Good heavens, no, Jenna. How could I forget for even one minute how you feel about the Sheltons!"

Jenna knew she'd hit a nerve. "Well, good," she said. "Because my feelings aren't about to change." She almost had to bite her tongue.

After Nate's visit the other night, she had to keep reminding herself that he was the last person she should trust. Or wonder about. Or lay awake nights, imagining what he was doing at the lighthouse.

"I just think you should give him and his plan a chance," Marion said. "I *think*," she added with forced calm, "that Nate hasn't given us a reason *not* to trust him."

Jenna stood, her hands fisted at her sides.

"Look, honey," Marion said. "I don't believe being a Shelton is an inherited disease. It's just a name." She smiled up at her daughter. "Give Nate a chance to prove himself to you—or not. I believe he's trying to do that."

Jenna let her fingers relax, and she sat back down. "It's hard for me to do."

"Of course. You loved your father, and I understand. But you've let everything else become wrapped up in that one night so many years ago."

"I have not."

"Oh, no? Then why won't you go to the lighthouse now?"

"I just don't want to." She looked at the floor. The truth was, she didn't think she could.

Marion stood and headed across the room. "Okay. I'm leaving. I'll see you in the morning. Have a nice time with George tonight."

She shut the door behind her, and Jenna stared at her nursing book. She had a few hours until the hardware store closed and George would pick her up. She should study. Her time was so precious. She stood, picked up her purse from the foyer table, glanced at her reflection in the mirror and went to her Jeep.

WITH ABOUT TWO HOURS of daylight left, Jenna drove out to the lake. When she turned onto the two-lane road that led to the lighthouse, her hands started perspiring. She rubbed first one and then the other on her jeans. "What are you going to do when you get there?" she said aloud. Maybe Nate wouldn't even be around. That would make her decision easy.

He was there. At least his truck was parked in front, so she assumed he was inside. She checked her rearview mirror. No one was behind her, so she took her foot off the accelerator and let the Jeep coast. She didn't spot Nate in the yard, and she couldn't see in the cottage windows from this far away. Her impulse was to drive on by.

She'd started to speed up again when she saw someone move in the large, south-facing window about three-quarters of the way up the beacon tower. Braking, she pulled off the road to get a better look. There were four windows at that elevation. The same figure appeared in the east window and stopped. Obviously Nate.

What was he doing? The stairs had been closed off years ago. They weren't safe.

He wore a blue shirt with the sleeves rolled up, and he had on a cap. His back was to the window and he appeared to be swinging a hammer. He stopped periodically to pull a nail from between his lips.

He was busy. Now wasn't a good time to approach. Her mind made up, she shifted into Drive. That's when she saw a wooden plank tumble from somewhere above Nate's head. He looked up, shouted an obscenity and covered his head, as dust floated down around him.

Jenna threw the Jeep in Park and jumped out. She ran up the crumbling sidewalk and yanked open the door. She hadn't been in the station since she was thirteen, but she hurried through the kitchen, hollering his name. "Nate! Are you all right?"

Hearing nothing but a rain of wood splinters, she noticed that the door to the beacon room, which had been padlocked for years, was open. Jenna stepped through and started up the stairs. "Nate! Answer me!"

A plank creaked above her. "I'm up here."

She exhaled and looked up. "I know that!"

She continued upward, making the sharp turns at the top of each staircase. She'd climbed three when she saw his face appear over the rickety handrail, which groaned with his weight.

"You're not supposed to be up there. The staircase was closed a long time ago by a building inspector," she panted.

He stepped away from the rail, took off his hat and slapped the brim against his thigh to remove dust. "I'm okay. I'm fixing the steps. I guess my hammering caused a weak board in the top level to give way. But heck, I got this far," he said.

For the first time in a very long time Jenna peered up to the top of the tower. She knew the bullet-riddled light had been hauled away years before after being destoyed by vandals. The windows lit the winding, cramped space Nate filled, sunshine turning his hair a deep golden bronze. Dust motes glittered as they swirled around him. Jenna felt as if she were staring up into a snow globe with Nate at its center.

"Come down from there right now," she said. "And be careful."

He obliged, following her slowly down the steps. When they reached the bottom, she moved out of his way to let him pass.

He tossed his cap on the kitchen table, rubbed the back of his hand over his mouth and finished by picking splinters off the tip of his tongue. "It's really cool up there," he said. "I remember the view, of course, and it hasn't changed, but I'd forgotten how peaceful and quiet the world seems when you're that high."

"Right," she said. "Peaceful with the sound of hammering, not to mention boards falling down around you."

"Well, except for that." He poured a glass of water and offered it to her. When she shook her head, he gulped it down. "It's kind of dusty."

"You shouldn't be up there," she stated. "It's dangerous."

He grinned at her. "You were worried about me?"

She felt her face flush. "I'd be worried about any idiot who was up in the tower by himself."

"Maybe so, but I was the idiot today, so don't spoil my moment." He opened his refrigerator. "Want something else to drink? I had beer but my brother drank them all."

She took the Coke he offered and popped the tab. "Mike was here?" A significant clue. His brother was high on her list of possible motives for Nate to buy the lighthouse.

"Yep. He showed me how to fix the stairs." Nate had a grin on his face, and it seemed as if it wasn't going to fade.

"What are you smiling about?" she demanded.

"You. Here." He looked around the kitchen. "I'm surprised, that's all."

Feeling dizzy, she pulled out a chair and sat. His simple statement made her realize the step she'd taken. She'd rushed right into the lighthouse without even thinking. She definitely hadn't been ready to step over the threshold, but now she was here, inside. Her heart rate jumped a couple of notches.

He leaned over to peer at her face. "You okay? You look pale."

She felt sick. Her hands trembled. She set the cola can down. All her senses suddenly became sharper. She breathed in the familiar smell she'd always associated with the light station—a mixture of water, brine and must. She heard the waves outside the back door, relentless against the giant boulders. They used to be soothing for her, but not now. Not since she'd rushed in the door and over the spot where…

She forced her mind to shut down, and supported her forehead in her right hand. "Actually, I've been better," she said.

"Let me get you some ice. I don't know why, but it seems like it's what you do when someone's close to fainting."

She glared at him. "I'm not going to faint. I might throw up, but I'll give you plenty of warning. Did it occur to you that it could be a little difficult for me to be in this building?"

He brought her a glass of ice anyway, and she poured her Coke over it. He sat across from her, and seemed genuinely concerned. "When was the last time you were here?"

"Not since—" she waved her hand in the air "—then."

"Oh, damn. Jeez, Jenna, I'm sorry. No wonder you want to…"

She snapped her attention to his face. He knew she wanted to tear down the building? "Want to what?"

"…throw up."

She nodded. "I don't *want* to throw up. Besides, I think the feeling is passing." It was, but now her knees were knocking together under the table. She felt as if the air was being squeezed from her lungs. "Look, I can't talk now. You talk about something. I'll listen."

"Okay. What?"

"I don't know. Your movies. Have I ever seen one?"

"You might have. I wrote a romantic comedy a couple of years ago when I was in my Neil Simon adulation stage. It was titled *Weekends at the Buzz* and was sort of an updated *You've Got Mail*. It was about three couples who regularly met at a Venice Internet café called, appropriately enough, The Buzz."

"I did see that," she said. "It was good."

He smiled. "Not everyone thought so, but thanks. Most of my other scripts have been suspense thrillers or action movies. Not your thing, I would imagine."

"You'd be surprised. I see a lot of action flicks."

"Oh, right. The strapping Mr. Lockley would prefer those."

They remained silent a minute or two, each lost in thought. Jenna's attack of nerves had settled. She studied the small kitchen. "I can see you've made improvements already," she said.

"A few."

"Nate?"

He glanced at her uncomfortably.

"Why did you buy this place?"

He sat back in his chair, his gaze intent on her face. "I knew we'd get around to that."

"Are we ever going to get around to the answer?"

"I can tell you one reason," he said. "I've become a terrible writer recently."

She squinted at him. Right.

"I suppose I'm looking for my muse."

"Here, in a decrepit lighthouse?"

"You never know. I've found inspiration in some strange places. Besides, the physical labor is good for me. A change of pace."

"They don't have things to fix in California?"

He looked around. "Not like this. It's special."

"Yeah, sure it is." She stood, feeling an overwhelming need to be free of this place. "I'm going outside."

He rose. "Did I say something to upset you?"

"No more than usual. I'll be back in a few minutes."

She walked out of the cottage and headed for the

trees beyond the lighthouse. She used to love being up here on the first cool days of autumn, when the leaves had just started to turn.

And then vandals had destroyed the lens, and the town's maintenance crew had more urgent jobs than to keep the overgrown paths cleared for hikers. Nate and his friends had started coming out here in their pickups, and only a few people, Jenna included, returned every so often to collect the garbage.

"Damn you, Nate," she muttered under her breath. "Do you really believe that a coat of paint can hide what happened to my father?"

She walked through a break in the trees and stood on one of the boulders overlooking the lake. Waves crashed just below her feet. Wind whipped against her, tossing her hair. She looked back through the dense foliage but couldn't see the cottage. Only the tip of the tower was visible above the treetops, its whimsical cupola standing stories above the shoddily patched roof of the house. She'd never seen the light when it was working. The electronic navigational tower had replaced it before she was born.

"Boy, this sure brings back memories."

She hadn't heard Nate come through the woods, but suddenly he was there, behind her. He stood with his legs braced, hands on his hips, his gaze on the horizon. And her bitterness multiplied. "What memories are those, Nate?" she said.

"When I was a kid, this seemed like the only place I could go to find…" He stopped, looked down at the smooth rock under his feet. "I don't know. Some kind of peace, I suppose. I remember when I got my first truck. I used to come here to get away. These woods offered me the chance to cut loose from responsibility, I guess. Although now that I think back, maybe this was more a place to hide."

Jenna stared out over the water. She supposed Nate did have a reason to hide back then. His life hadn't been easy.

She heard his footsteps and knew he'd leaped onto the rock where she was standing. And then he put his hand over her shoulder. She stood there, stupidly letting the son of the man who'd killed her father comfort her. As if she needed comfort from Nate. So why didn't she move? Because his hand felt warm and strong and good….

He turned her around and looked into her eyes. "You seem like you belong here, Jenna. You belong because this place is a part of you." He wrapped his hand around the nape of her neck and pulled her gently toward him. When she instinctively turned her head aside, he stopped her. "Would you mind if I kissed you?"

She felt so torn, so uncertain. "Nate, don't…"

His lips brushed hers, lightly, like a breeze at dawn. Her heart pounded and her skin grew warm. But her mind was filled with the resentment that had sustained her for years. It was familiar. It defined her. She pushed against his chest.

He raised his hands in the air. "Okay."

Jenna stepped around him, her own hands shaking. And her lips tingling from that sweet, fleeting contact she feared could change her in ways she wasn't prepared for. She shot him a glance over her shoulder. "Let's forget it, okay?"

He watched her walk back through the woods, twigs snapping under her sneakers, branches whipping against her legs. Nate climbed down off the rocks and followed her, keeping distance between them. Why did he care so much about getting this woman to like him? She made it so damn hard. She'd harbored resentment toward his family, rightly or wrongly, for more years than a few weeks could erase. And yet he craved her approval.

He was never going to get it, and maybe he really didn't deserve it. He hadn't been honest with her about his motive for buying the lighthouse. For a while he'd convinced himself she was being so unreasonable that she didn't merit his honesty. But he didn't want to hurt her. She was already so wounded.

And he liked her too much. Nate slowed his steps. He was being stupid. He didn't need grief from a woman who was determined not to give him a break.

Maybe he was just caught up in this whole lighthouse—Jenna connection, and it was driving him a little nuts. What he needed was to write again. Ideas popped into his head all the time now that he was living at the station. None of them had gelled yet, but one would. The physical work was freeing his mind. Hell, maybe Jenna's stubborn determination fired his own.

But despite his best intentions, he'd quickened his pace again. "Go out with me tonight," he called.

She stopped, just for a second, and then kept walking. "No."

"Tomorrow night."

"I can't."

"Why not?"

She halted, glaring at him. "I date George, Nate. George. We're a thing, you know."

"You're engaged?"

"No. But we're sort of exclusive."

"You love him?" Damn. He sounded desperate.

She crossed her arms. "I'm very fond of him."

"Ah-ha!"

She made a frustrated sound very much like a growl and started walking again.

He'd missed this chance, but he was getting somewhere. It was a first step. But toward what? he wondered.

## CHAPTER TEN

GEORGE PULLED INTO Jenna's driveway at nine-thirty Saturday night and shut off his engine. They'd gone to dinner at the local seafood place and ended up back here. He turned in his seat. "You feeling any better?"

She'd complained of a headache. It wasn't a lie, exactly; she was close to having one. "A little."

He opened his door and started to get out, but she stopped him with a hand on his arm. "I'm tired, George. Is it okay if we call it a night?"

He looked at her, troubled. "I'm worried about you, Jen."

"Don't be. I've just got this crazy schedule."

"You don't get enough rest."

"I always catch up. Like now. I'm going right to bed. I'll probably sleep for ten hours."

"It's not just that. You haven't been yourself since Nate Shelton came here. I can sense your tension. That guy's pushing all your buttons."

That was an understatement. "Don't worry. I can handle Nate. But I am disappointed in having to give up my plans for the lighthouse." She smiled, hoping to reassure George. "My disappointment isn't Nate's fault. The property was for sale. I just didn't get the money together soon enough."

She stared out the window of his truck. Wow. What she'd just said was logical. Maybe she was starting to accept the inevitable.

"I don't like the guy, Jen. I don't trust him. It's not just the things you've told me about his family. He's slick. He's always coming up with these smart answers, as if he doesn't owe anything to anybody."

Jenna thought about that. "What *does* he owe anybody, George?"

"He owes you, that's for sure. His father killed yours, and Nate ran away without trying to help make things right."

"He moved out of town. That's all. Finnegan Cove wasn't good for him back then."

George released her hand. "You're defending the guy now? What's going on?"

"Nothing," she answered, much too quickly. "I'm just tired." She lay her hand on his shoulder. "I'm going in. I'll talk to you tomorrow."

He reached across her and grabbed the door handle. "Marry me, Jenna. Let me take care of you."

"What?" She felt dizzy, but not from joy. Why did he have to bring this up again now? "Oh, George. I don't need a protector."

His eyes clouded over. "I didn't mean it like that. I just meant that I make good money. You can be a nurse, of course, but if we become engaged, you can stop working at the bakery. You can tell Nate to take a flying leap…."

So that was it. At least the reason behind *this* proposal. Jenna knew George loved her. She was grateful. But she realized she'd never returned those feelings in the same measure. She'd been so unfair to him.

"Can we talk about this later? My thoughts aren't clear right now. I just need to go inside and—"

He jerked away from her and looked out his side window. "Go on then."

She opened her door and got out. "I'll call you," she said, leaning in.

Without looking at her, he said, "Shut the door, Jen."

When she did, he slammed the truck into gear and peeled out of her driveway.

She stood for a moment watching his taillights fade. "You handled that beautifully, Jenna," she said.

NORMALLY NATE WAS a pretty rational guy. He didn't have mood swings or emotional highs and lows like many so-called creative people. And even if once in a blue moon he did behave in a way that might be considered out of the ordinary, he lived in Los Angeles. *Ordinary* wasn't a word a person heard around L.A. But this was Finnegan Cove, and he supposed stalking Jenna Malloy might raise some eyebrows.

Of course, Nate didn't consider his actions as stalking, exactly. More appropriately, he was conducting a drive-by snoop, and that wasn't anywhere close to sinister.

He drove by Jenna's house for the first time about nine-fifteen Saturday night.

*Why the hell are you doing this?* he wondered as he turned onto Hummingbird for his third pass half an hour later. He didn't think he was fixated on Jenna simply because she didn't want him. He'd been turned down by women before and hadn't acted all crazy.

And he wasn't a particularly prideful man. He'd had experience with rejection. Just this week, Brendan Willis from Boneyard Films had called to say Nate's latest script didn't "fit the Boneyard profile" right now. Big surprise. Still, no rejection was easy to take, but he was having a hard time accepting Jenna's opinion of him.

Jenna was smart and funny. She was cute and sexy and didn't seem to know it. He enjoyed being with her. And he was thinking about her entirely too much.

If he could just get past this lighthouse dilemma. Once she discovered that Harley was coming back, and Nate had known…

An all-too-familiar ache assailed him. He rotated his neck in an effort to relieve tense muscles. They refused to unknot. That's the way it was with guilt. He'd never been very good at ignoring it.

He knew he had to tell Jenna about Harley. And

he would, just not now. Not when he needed to sort out his feelings for her. If she truly hated him, if she'd never get over the death of her father, then waiting a few days, a week, wouldn't matter.

A tan pickup truck roared by him. Nate slowed to a crawl and tried to see inside the cab. The driver looked like George Lockley, and he seemed mad as hell. Nate sped toward Jenna's and stopped a couple of houses away. He saw her at her front door. She seemed okay. He looked at his watch: 9:45. "You're an idiot," he told himself. "Go home."

But he didn't. He got out of his truck and headed to her front door. The television was on. He knocked.

Jenna peeked through the curtain of her window. Nate waved. She opened the door. "What are you doing here?"

He leaned against the door frame. "You ask me that a lot."

"Yes, because it's a logical question, don't you think?"

"I suppose. You going to invite me in?"

"Not now, Nate."

He didn't move. "How was your date with George?"

"You care about that?"

"I noticed you didn't invite him in."

"You were watching?"

"I just saw him rocket out of here. Something happen?"

"That's none of your business, and anyway, it's late."

He tapped his wristwatch. "It's not even ten o'clock."

She started to close the door, but he propped it open with his elbow. "I was thinking maybe it was because of me."

She pulled the door open again. "I didn't invite him in because of you? Why would I turn away my boyfriend because of a man I've just discovered is a voyeur?"

Nate smiled. He thought about explaining his drive-by snooping to her, but wisely didn't. "So dependable ol' George didn't *want* to come in?"

She leaned against the door and sighed. "Nate, this is much too personal."

"You're right. Let's go for a ride."

"Absolutely not." But her eyes betrayed her. He waited. "Where?" she finally said.

"I know the perfect place."

"Why would we—" she pointed her finger at him, then at herself "—go for a ride on a Saturday night? We barely even like each other."

"That's only half-true. I like you. I'd like the chance to change your mind about me."

She started tapping her foot, as if maybe she was considering. So he pressed harder. "Just a short ride. You'll be home in an hour."

She released a great, put-upon sigh. "One hour. Let me turn off the television and get my keys."

She walked ahead of him without speaking and got in his truck. He backed out, drove down Hummingbird to Main Street, retracing his earlier path. Then he turned toward the lighthouse. He was following a hunch. One that would work out just fine if he'd written it into a script.

AFTER FIVE MINUTES Jenna had the route figured out. "Oh, great. We're going to my favorite place."

But she didn't care. The night was cool. She had to admit the guy was interesting. And she'd been feeling lousy about the way her date with George had ended. She wasn't keen on sitting in her living room debating her insensitivity.

She sat quietly as Nate pulled into the gravel lot. He turned sharply to the left, toward the woods. His headlights speared the screen of trees.

"You can't drive in there."

"Why not?"

"There's no road."

"Got four-wheel drive." Slowing, he headed among the trees, the truck lurching on the uneven ground. "It is a bit more overgrown than I thought, though."

Jenna held tight to the door handle. "What do you think you're doing?"

"Reliving our youths. You used to go to the woods, didn't you?"

She had, a few times. But she was certain her occasional dates were nothing like Nate's. "I think our teenage experiences were quite different."

He didn't respond. Branches brushed against the

side of the truck. "You're going to scratch the finish on this rental vehicle," she pointed out.

"It's not your problem. Can't you just sit back and enjoy the ride?"

She bounced off her seat as the vehicle jolted. "Sure. This is superenjoyable. Don't know when I've ever had a better time."

He looked over at her and raised his right eyebrow. "Jenna, zip it. We're almost there."

He drove perhaps another quarter mile to the lake, where he stopped in front of a break in the boulder wall. His lights fanned over the water lapping at the shoreline. He cut the engine and crossed his arms over the steering wheel. Staring out at Lake Michigan, he said, "I used to imagine I could see all the way to Wisconsin, and maybe a kid in his truck in Milwaukee could see my headlights."

The water, rippling in shades of black and silver, stretched under a canopy of very bright stars. "It's nice here," Jenna said. "Perfect for whatever you did on those weekend nights." She hoped the look she gave him indicated that his subtle charm wasn't fooling her.

He chuckled before giving her a smile that was warm and natural in the soft light coming from the dashboard. "What I did then was no different from what I'm planning to do now," he said. "With a couple of exceptions."

Surprised by a tingling anticipation, Jenna said, "What are you talking about?"

He took a CD out of a leather wallet and slipped it into the player. "Back then my truck only had a radio, and sometimes it didn't work. Now I'm high tech." The harmonious crooning of contemporary country music filled the cab. "Back then I listened to Jefferson Airplane. Now, Brooks and Dunn." He reached behind the driver's seat, popped the lid on a cooler and brought out a bottle of white wine with a screw top. "Back then," he said, "beer from a can. Now—" he removed two glasses and handed her one "—an exceptional 2007 chardonnay purchased one hour ago at the Pick 'n Save."

He poured the wine. Jenna gripped the stem of her glass tightly and chewed her lip. Why didn't she stop him? She would in a while.

He poured himself a glass and took a swallow. "But this isn't all that's different," he said.

"Oh, no? What else?"

He patted the dashboard. "Better truck." He looked into her eyes. "And definitely better girl."

She swallowed, sucked in a quick, panicky breath. And almost slipped off the edge of the seat. Nate had been on this beautiful shoreline maybe a hundred nights with who knew how many different girls. And Jenna had only been here in her dreams....

He pointed at her wine. "Go ahead. It's top-shelf Finnegan Cove."

She took a sip, waited a moment and said, "I can see where this is headed, Nate, and—"

"Can you?" He settled back in his seat. "Do you

know that I'll probably wait through another song or two, watch the water, talk with you awhile? Then my hand is going to make its way to your shoulder. My fingers will lightly stroke your neck. Then I'm going to set down this glass and reach for yours..."

She closed her eyes, seeing his hand, feeling his touch, before he ever moved. She opened her eyes and looked at him. "Nate, we shouldn't...."

He turned toward her. "Why, Jenna? Because you've convinced yourself that you don't like me? I know you hated me once. I understand that. And I know you're trying to hate me now. But you can't. So this kiss that's been lingering in the air between us is going to happen."

His fingers snaked under her hair and feathered over the nape of her neck. Goose bumps rose on her skin. He put his glass in the cup holder, then did the same with hers. "I've thought about this long enough. Let's live dangerously. It's time to know what it's like to kiss you and what you think it's like to kiss me."

He inched over on the seat and pulled her closer. "I have a hunch it's going to be good. But if you don't think it is, I'll take you home, and on Monday I'll congratulate George. He won't know what for, but I will."

She laid her hand on Nate's chest, a token gesture. Her resistance was all but gone. "And you and me? What will Monday be like for us? This will change things."

"Maybe." He pulled a strand of hair over her shoulder and stroked it between his thumb and finger. "But worst-case scenario—after tonight, if you're still working on that hate thing, Monday will be like the days before this one. And I'll always wonder what it would have been like if our pasts had been different."

The memories of those differences had been haunting Jenna ever since Nate had showed up in the bakery over a week ago. But now, with his hand caressing her neck, all she could think about was what would happen if she liked the kiss. Could it make her forget what Harley had done? And what about when Nate went back to California? What would this moment have been for?

He cupped her cheek. "Jenna, you're thinking. This is about feeling." He leaned in, pressed his lips to hers, softly, just like he had in her imagination.

Her shoulders sagged as she clenched her hand to keep from reaching for him. He moved his mouth over hers and swept his tongue along the line of her lips. She opened to him, and he probed her mouth with a shattering intensity. When his arm went around her, she moaned and let him pull her to him, and thought about how wonderful it was when a grown woman's reality surpassed the dreams of a young girl.

And then the kiss changed. It became hotter, needier. Nate massaged her back, his hand disappearing under her top and moving up her spine. He kissed her for long, exquisite moments.

When their lips parted, he didn't break contact. He nuzzled her neck, breathing deeply, nipping at her earlobe. She arched back, giving him access to her throat. His mouth made a soft, sucking sound and left a moist trail to her collarbone. Her breasts tingled. Eyelids fluttering, she caught glimpses of his sandy hair in the soft-yellow light. With one finger he pulled down her knit top to let his tongue explore the swell of flesh above her bra.

"That's...that's more than a kiss, Nate." Her voice came from somewhere deep in her throat.

His mouth moved over her heated skin, pressing urgent kisses between her breasts. "I suppose technically it is," he mumbled.

She drew away and fell back against the passenger seat. To keep from releasing the shuddering breath that would reveal more than she wanted him to know, she bit the inside of her cheek. After a moment he moved over to his seat. "I'm certainly interested in your opinion of that, but I have to tell you, Jenna, for me it was spectacular. In fact, I can see myself doing it again real soon."

She smoothed her pants. "Did it bring back memories?"

He smiled. "No, ma'am. Nothing compared." He handed her the glass of wine. She sipped at it, grateful to have something to do.

"I like modern necking," he said. "Now what are we going to do about it?"

"Take me home."

"Yours or mine?" He nodded toward the woods. "I'm only asking because mine is just through there, about a half mile."

She shot him a cool look despite an internal spike in temperature that she felt all the way to her toes. "Mine."

He started the engine. "Good. Yours has more amenities."

"I'm going in alone."

He tightened his hand around the gear shift. "I was afraid you'd say that."

Ten minutes later she got out of his truck. He rolled down the window. "You never said. How was it?"

She smiled wryly, realizing that she'd never felt more like grinning in her life. "If you have to ask, you weren't paying attention."

He gave her a thumbs-up. "You see, we can agree on something."

## CHAPTER ELEVEN

NINE DAYS HAD PASSED since Nate last saw his father. So he wasn't surprised at the anticipation he felt when he pulled into the parking lot of the correctional facility at noon on Sunday. In less than three weeks Harley would be released, and Nate had so much to tell him. The lighthouse was improving every day. But more importantly, he and Jenna were getting along, and Nate actually hoped she might believe him when he told her his father had changed. That would pave the way for Jenna to accept Harley's plans for living quietly in the lighthouse.

Nate parked, got out of his car and was walking toward the visitors' entrance when he spotted a woman across the lot. He watched her a moment and then recognized her by the short curly hair.

"Marion!"

She stopped and stared, and her purse slipped out of her hand. He heard her gasp despite the two rows of parked cars separating them.

When he reached her, he bent to pick up her pockettbook. "Marion, what are you doing here?"

She grabbed her purse. "Nate…I should be asking you that question."

He tried to smile though the situation was bizarre. Was she kidding? "You wonder why I'm here? My father is in prison here."

Her hand flattened against her chest. "Oh, yes, of course. I remember now. I suppose that had slipped my mind."

She failed to remember where her husband's convicted murderer was imprisoned? Nate shook his head. Her nervousness suggested a grim possibility to him—that she'd been informed by the parole board that Harley was scheduled for release, and was here today to argue that decision. That would explain her reluctance to tell the truth.

Marion's face had paled dramatically. "Are you all right?" he asked in concern.

"Yes. I was just leaving."

"But why *are* you here?" he repeated.

"I…uh…I came to take an order for the bakery."

"An order? The prison buys from you all the way in Finnegan Cove?"

"Yes. Rolls. They buy dinner rolls." She stared down at her purse. "It's very lucrative for my shop. I make hundreds of them."

Nate almost laughed. Foggy Creek housed over fifteen hundred inmates. Surely the facility had ovens to produce dinner rolls.

She stepped away from him. "I really have to go, Nate."

"Oh. Sure. I'll see you back in town."

"Yes, well, goodbye." She made an effort to smile, then turned and walked away from him.

He watched her cross the lot. When she stuck her key into the door of her small car, she looked back. "I would appreciate it if you didn't tell Jenna you saw me," she called. "The profit I make is sort of my mad money." She made a high-pitched, nervous sound. "A woman's got to have her little secrets," she added.

*I'll bet.* Only this wasn't a *little* secret. Nate waved noncommittally. "Drive carefully."

He considered other possible scenarios that might account for Marion's appearance today. But ultimately, if she hadn't come to plead to keep his father locked up, he could only think of one reason why she would come to Foggy Creek—to visit someone here. He doubted she knew any of the employees at the facility. The prison was far enough from Finnegan Cove that the staff wouldn't live anywhere near the town. And he could only imagine one inmate Marion could possibly know.

When his father came into the visitors' room, Nate stood. "What a treat," Harley said, beaming. "Seeing you again so soon."

"I wanted to report on the lighthouse," Nate told him.

"Good. I'm anxious to hear."

Both men sat at the table. "Before I go into that," Nate said, "I have to tell you who I just ran into in the parking lot."

Harley's back stiffened. "Who…who was that?"

"Marion Malloy, of all people." He waited for a response, but all Harley did was drum his fingers on the table. "Isn't that strange?" Nate pressed.

His dad cleared his throat. "I'll say. Strange."

"She said she was here taking an order for her bakery."

Harley nodded, his gaze fixed on his fingers. "I suppose that's possible."

"What does she do, Dad? Bake cakes with files in them to pass around to the inmates?"

Harley forced a chuckle. "I doubt that. At least I never got one."

"Did you see her when she was here?"

"Me? I'd be the last person she'd want to visit."

"That's what I thought." Nate propped his elbows on the table and leaned forward. "Come clean, Dad. Why was Marion here?"

"How would I—?"

"I want the truth. Marion was here about you, wasn't she? Did someone from the prison call her about your parole hearing?"

Harley expelled a long breath. "Yes, that's exactly it. I didn't want to upset you. The warden called her and she hightailed it out here to ask me not to come back. She wants me to live somewhere other than the lighthouse—somewhere outside of Finnegan cove."

Nate cupped his hand over his mouth and stared at his father. He didn't buy it. Harley was providing too much information. "So have you decided not to move back? Do you want me to sell the station?"

Harley knitted his eyebrows, frowning. "I wouldn't be too hasty. Marion's a nice lady. I think she'll adjust to the idea once I settle in." He shook his head. "I don't expect it'll be a problem."

Nate was used to reading between the lines, and this dialogue seemed to demand it. "You know, Dad," he said, affecting a casual tone, "you're right. Marion is a nice lady. But I'm wondering how you know that. In fact, I'm wondering how well you know Mrs. Malloy after all these years."

"I remember her from before. She was always kind to me."

Nate stared hard into his eyes. "Dad, I've got to know that you're being truthful with me. Did Marion come to see you?"

Harley looked down, took a deep breath. When he raised his face, a vein throbbed in his temple. "This isn't the first time she's come, Nate. Marion has been a regular visitor." He paused a moment before saying, "Marion and you have gotten me through this."

"Marion has been visiting you all this time?"

Harley nodded.

"Why?"

He didn't answer. The capillaries in his cheeks reddened, telling Nate what he wanted to know. He felt as if he'd been sucker punched. "No, Dad. Not you and Marion?"

Harley still didn't speak.

"But that doesn't make sense. She started coming here after you were convicted of killing Joe? Why would she do that?"

Harley crossed his arms. "There's a history between us. That's all I'm saying on the subject."

"History? You mean from before Joe died?"

"I'm not telling you any more, Nathaniel. This is private."

"But, Dad, if you were seeing Marion while Joe was alive, that changes everything…."

"It changes nothing, son. Nothing."

"But the prosecutor during the trial said that you and Joe argued over fishing rights. No one questioned that as the motive. You and Joe had been competitors for years."

"That's right. We argued about territory. It got rough. I hit Joe with that board and killed him. That's the way it happened."

"That might be the *way* it happened, but it's not *why* it happened."

Harley leaned forward. "Don't stir things up, Nate. I've served my time. It's over. And Marion is a good and moral woman. I won't have her reputation sullied."

Nate sat for long uncomfortable moments, letting that sink in. His father and Marion. And no one knew. Or if anyone did, no one had told. Not even…Nate forced the next words out of his parched throat. "Does Jenna know about this *history* between you and her mother?"

"No. And that's the way it has to be for now."

The horrifying consequences of this secret suddenly became clear to Nate. "You're being released soon. You're going back to the town where everyone thinks you're a murderer—"

"I am a murderer, Nate. Tried and convicted."

"Let me finish. You're planning to take up with the widow of the man you killed? The man Jenna is still grieving?" He shook his head, trying to clear his thoughts. "What are you and Marion thinking? Jenna has to be told before you come back! This will devastate her."

Harley rubbed his chin with his thumb. "I agree with you, but it's not up to me to tell her." He pointed at Nate. "And it's not up to you. It's not our secret to tell."

Nate couldn't argue. He didn't want to tell Jenna. They were just getting started. He liked her too much. "Marion has to do it," he stated.

"I've told her that. For years I've urged her to be honest with her daughter. Now she has to. She knows that."

Nate stared down at the top of the table, but didn't see the faint gray grain of the surface, worn pale by countless hands. He thought about Jenna last night in the truck. He'd tossed in bed all night, eager to see her again today. Jenna was real, honest, even harsh in her forthrightness—qualities he admired after all the games people played in L.A.

He hadn't felt this way about anyone in years. How could he face her now that he knew a secret that could destroy her faith in her mother. And in the Sheltons, once again?

"I know you're working at the station despite Jenna's protests," Harley said, breaking into his thoughts. "I appreciate that. Maybe you're the person who can take away some of the pain she feels when she thinks of that place."

Hester had said almost the same thing. Again, Nate didn't like this role that had been assigned to him.

"You're a good man, Nate," Harley said. "And I need you to be patient just a little longer."

*A good man? I've kept the reason I bought the lighthouse from Jenna. And now you're asking me to keep this from her, an even more damaging truth.*

Harley seemed oblivious to Nate's battle with his conscience. "You can't tell her about Marion and me. Her mother will do it soon. She knows Jenna better than anyone. She'll tell her in a gentle way."

"It's not right, Dad."

"Maybe not, son, but I won't give up what time I've got left, and Marion wants to stay in Finnegan Cove. I love her, and I want to be with her. I have to trust her to do what she thinks is best."

Nate stood. He couldn't deny that his father deserved some peace. Happiness. "I've got to go, Dad. I need to think." He walked around the table and stopped beside his father.

His dad looked up at him, his expression sad and worried. "You're coming to see me again, aren't you?"

"Yeah."

Unseasonably warm sunshine pressed on Nate's back as he walked to his truck. Like the guilt on his shoulders. Two and a half weeks ago he'd found out about his father's parole. All he'd wanted was to help him get a new start. And now, as luck would have it, Nate was falling for the one woman who stood to be hurt by his deception.

NATE TOOK A DETOUR on his way back to town. He couldn't risk running into Jenna today. He couldn't face her until he sorted this mess out. He followed the coast, stopping occasionally to stare out over the water, hoping for a solution to come to him. And then he ended up in Sutter's Point, with his cell phone in his hand. He punched in the new number he'd recently added.

His brother answered. "Nate. Is something wrong?"

Nate tried to sound cheerful, but knew when bad acting was just that. Bad acting. "Can you spare a few minutes? Meet me somewhere?"

"There's a place on the outskirts of town on the old coast road. Called Bert's Grill. Meet me there."

"Okay."

Fifteen minutes later, Nate sat at a table on the crowded patio of a bar and grill that smelled like suntan oil, garlic and freshwater crabs. The combination brought back memories. When he saw Mike come in, he motioned him over and ordered two beers.

As he sat down across from his brother, Mike asked him, "What happened? You look like hell."

"I just came from Foggy Creek."

"Enough said. That would ruin my appetite, too."

"No. You don't understand. I learned something there today."

"Okay. Tell me. Not that anything would surprise me."

Nate paused while the waitress set two bottles and two frosted glasses on the table. Then he poured his beer and took a long drink. "I saw Marion Malloy at the prison. It seems our father and Jenna's mother have a relationship that's been going on since even before Joe was killed."

Mike stared, his own bottle pressed against his lips as if frozen there. Then he slowly lowered his beer to the table. "I was wrong. That surprises me. How can you have a relationship when you're in jail?"

"Beats me," Nate said. "I didn't get the details, but apparently it's possible. Anyway, Dad's going to Finnegan Cove to take up where he left off before he was convicted."

"That stupid old bastard."

Nate didn't agree, but he didn't argue, either.

"Does Jenna know?" Mike asked.

He shook his head. "And when she finds out, she'll be really hurt. She hates Dad, and I can't fault her for that. She only remembers him the way he was—rough, angry, drunk eighty percent of the time. She doesn't know him now—the guy proves that rehabilitation is possible."

Mike smirked. "That's your opinion, little bro. I don't buy it."

Nate tried to tamp a rising anger. "You haven't even bothered to see him, Mike. How would you know what he's like?"

His brother tapped the top of his beer bottle against his temple. "I've got a memory, Nate. A mean old man like Harley can't change."

"You left," Nate reminded him. "If you'd stayed around, you'd have seen what I did. Dad started to change a few months before the…the incident at the lighthouse. He was becoming gentler, kinder. He'd cut down on the drinking."

"A real saint, huh?"

"No, but a decent man."

Mike turned his bottle in his big hands. "And you credit Marion Malloy with this miracle?"

"It's possible. I can't think of any other explanation for Dad's turnaround. That's why his violent act that night was more than disappointing. It was baffling. I couldn't understand how Dad could have committed this crime."

"I hate to destroy your innocent faith in the power of love, Nate, but it's bull. The man I remember—"

"Isn't the man he is now," Nate insisted.

Mike gave him a cunning sort of smile. "Okay. Let's say you're right. Let's say the old man has had an epiphany or something. Still, this new, improved Harley has been harboring this secret for years. And he's going back to the town where everybody hates him, just so he can be with his lover. Doesn't matter that he's about to destroy her daughter. Doesn't matter that he's involved you with his lies." Mike took a swallow. "Oh, yeah. The man's a prince."

Nate let out a long breath. "I can't defend him to you, Mike. You're never going to forgive him for the way he treated you after Mom died."

"Damn straight."

"But he has changed. He doesn't take any pleasure from this situation. He's tried to get Marion to tell Jenna the truth, but she hasn't."

"Bottom line, Nate," Mike said, "are you going to tell her?"

"Dad asked me not to. He says it's Marion's secret, her place to tell it."

"My opinion…and I assume that's why you're here today, because you want it…Harley's right. I just pray Marion tells her before she finds out on her own."

"That's the truly frightening part," Nate said. "I feel like I'm playing with a time bomb. It's bad enough that I haven't told Jenna why I bought the lighthouse. Now I know this, and I wish to God I didn't."

"And why, exactly, haven't you told her about the lighthouse?" Mike asked.

Nate went over in his mind all the justifications he'd been telling himself for days. But after last night, he'd come to the only conclusion he could. "I was going to tell her today. And hope it didn't finish what we've got. But now…"

Mike smiled, a more genuine expression. "So you've got something with Jenna?"

"I like her, Mike. I haven't known her that long, but she stirs something in me. She comes across as this strong, independent woman on the outside, but she's vulnerable under the surface. I feel almost protective of her—more so now that I know." Nate drained the last of his beer. "But here's the thing…any chance that Jenna might continue to warm to me will be impossible after she hears this."

Nate raised his hand. The waitress crossed the busy room and stopped at their table. He ordered two more beers. "I want to keep seeing Jenna," he said, "though with us living two thousand miles apart, it doesn't seem practical."

"Feelings aren't ever practical," Mike said, grinning. "Look at mine for Dad. Gut emotion all the way." He sat back in the chair and remained thoughtful a few moments.

"I wish Wendy was here. My wife knows a lot more about relationship stuff than I do, or want to."

Nate would have appreciated a woman's viewpoint, as well. In California, as a writer, he prided himself on being something of an expert in human emotions and motivations. He managed to make audiences believe he knew what he was doing when he fictionalized people's behavior. But when the emotional stuff happened to him, that was a different story. He felt clueless.

"We're at a standstill here," Mike said. "I hate to ask so bluntly, but have you and Jenna…you know?"

"No." Nate smiled. "But not for lack of trying on my part."

"That's good. Simplifies the situation. I think the smartest thing you could do now is put some distance between you. At least until Marion tells Jenna. If you don't, if you encourage this, and Jenna discovers what you've been hiding, then you won't have a chance in hell."

"I have to at least tell her why I bought the station."

"I could argue that either way," Mike said. "I just know one thing for sure. The fact that you bought the lighthouse for Harley isn't as damaging as the knowledge of this relationship that's been going on for years. You didn't know how your decision would affect Jenna when you made the trip from California. But what Marion's been doing…that's pretty indefensible. And you're a part of it now, whether you want to be or not."

Nate knew his brother was right. But how would Jenna feel when he didn't contact her, flirt with her, kiss her again? Hell, how would he feel, not being able to do those things?

"Are you buying dinner?" Mike said. "They have great hot wings at this place."

"Sure, why not?" Nate didn't figure a case of indigestion could make a bad situation worse.

The brothers talked together throughout the meal, and parted shortly after dark. At least one good thing had come out of this emotional disaster, Nate figured as he drove back to town. He was getting to know Mike again.

# CHAPTER TWELVE

JENNA ARRIVED at the bakery at 6:00 a.m. on Monday. Her mother was busy in the kitchen, but she turned when Jenna came through the swinging door. "Hi."

"Hey, Mom. How was your day off? Do anything interesting?"

Marion's shoulders seemed to sag. She set a tray of pastries on the counter. "You okay?" Jenna asked.

"Sure. Fine." She occupied herself by arranging croissants on a crockery platter. "Did you see Nate yesterday?"

"No. He didn't call. I don't know where he was."

Marion kept her eyes on her task. "Does he have your number?"

"It's in the book. He could have reached me. If he'd wanted to."

"Maybe he's just preoccupied, working on the station," her mom suggested.

"Maybe." Jenna had been disappointed and confused when Nate didn't call her after Saturday night. She and Valerie had met at Mickey's for supper on Sunday. Jenna had confessed everything to her, including her guilt over the way she'd handled things with George. Valerie had been understanding, and the two of them tried to come up with a reason why Nate had been a no-show all day. Jenna was still wondering as she took the platter of croissants from her mother.

*Isn't it obvious?* she thought as she entered the dining area of the bakery and checked the display cases. *Nate hasn't changed.*

Marion came out of the kitchen, filled the basket of one of the coffee brewers and set it to drip. After a moment, she said, "I've got an errand to run this morning. I'll have to leave you alone here for a while."

"No problem. I'll manage."

Marion looked at Jenna and rubbed her hands on her apron. "So you don't have any plans to see Nate?"

"I told you. I don't know where he is. After I leave here, I'll just go home."

"I thought you and he were becoming close," she said.

Jenna set a full coffeepot on the warmer and an empty one on the machine. "Apparently not."

"Okay then," Marion said. "I'll run my errand just as soon as the morning rush is over." She turned abruptly and disappeared into the kitchen.

Jenna stared after her. Her mother was acting strangely. Wasn't everyone?

NATE HEARD A CAR ENGINE, and saw from the window with both relief and regret that it wasn't Jenna's Jeep.

He set down his drill as he watched Marion pull her small car around the side of the station and park, then went out to meet her. "Good morning, Marion."

She walked quickly toward him. "Harley called me. He said you know everything."

Nate released a bark of laughter. "Right. I have a feeling I don't know the half of it. But about you and my dad, yeah, I know what's been going on." He opened the door for her and she stepped inside, where he gestured to a kitchen chair.

"I don't need to sit," she said, instead leaning against the counter. "Thanks for not telling Jenna that you saw me at Foggy Creek."

"Don't thank me. I don't agree with keeping this from her."

"I know. Neither does your father."

"You've already waited at least twenty years too long, Marion." Her face blanched, but Nate couldn't feel much sympathy for her.

"I love your father, Nate. I've loved him since before…"

He waited. If she thought he would make this easy on her, she was mistaken. And if she thought that last statement made everything okay, she was wrong again.

"He's not the murderer everyone believes him to be."

Now she had his attention. "Are you saying he didn't kill Joe?"

She shook her head. "No. He did kill Joe, but you don't know all the facts."

"You want to enlighten me?"

"Yes, but not until I tell Jenna everything."

Great. "Before or after my dad's parole? Before he arrives back in the town where he's a convicted murderer?" At least two questions had been cleared up for Nate. He now understood why his father was so determined to return to Finnegan Cove. And why he'd begun to show some signs of his former humanity before he murdered Joe.

"People won't think that once they get to know Harley again. Once they see the man that you and I know, they won't hate him."

"For Pete's sake, Marion, wake up. Your own daughter hates him, and with good reason."

Marion fisted her hand over her chest. "You don't think that breaks my heart every day, Nate? I love Jenna, and I haven't been able to tell her about the most important relationship in my life, next to the one I have with her."

He looked into her eyes and tried to find compassion in his heart. Nope. Wasn't there.

She held out her hand, but didn't move to touch him. "Just bear with me. I will tell her. When I know how to…." She searched his face. "Don't you see, Nate? Everybody involved in this situation wants to do the right thing."

"Gee, Marion, if that's true, how come nobody has?" He crossed his arms and stated the sad truth, "Including me. If you don't tell her pretty damn soon, I will. She'll probably hate me, but I'll take that chance."

He went to the door and opened it. "For now, we're done. But I'm warning you, don't take too long."

FOR THE NEXT THREE DAYS Nate tried to occupy his mind with work. Every night he sat staring at the story ideas he'd put into his computer. And then without coming up with any new material, he'd shut off the machine and watch a DVD from Cove Video Rental. Fine thing. A man sitting all alone on his new sofa, watching movies, when he should be writing them.

By Thursday night he figured he'd waited long enough. Marion obviously hadn't told her daughter yet. He hadn't been to the bakery for his morning coffee. Jenna hadn't come to the lighthouse. He hadn't called her or been to her house. Damn it. He missed her. He'd put enough of that so-called emotional distance Mike had talked about between him and Jenna. It was time to see where he stood.

When he was sure she'd be home from class, he got into his truck and headed for Hummingbird Street. What if she wasn't back yet? Worse, what if George was there?

That was a no-brainer; obviously Nate would turn around and go home.

But the lights were on and only Jenna's Jeep was in the drive, so he pulled in and went to her door. He knocked. When she looked out the window, her eyes registered shock and something else Nate didn't want to think about. She hollered through the glass, "I'm busy."

He heard her television in the background. "You're watching TV."

"Yes. I'm busy watching TV."

"Come on, Jenna. Open the door. If you don't want to invite me in, that's okay. I'll state my purpose for being here and leave."

She dropped the curtain back over the window, and a moment later opened the door a few inches. "What are you doing here?" she asked.

He smiled. "There's that question again."

"And isn't it especially appropriate now?"

"I came to explain."

The door remained solidly in his path. He could only see half her face. "Okay. Explain."

"I'm actually prepared with several explanations. I'm wondering which one you'd like to hear first."

Her expression never changed. "Let's start with the one about you talking me into going to the woods with you on Saturday night. Then we can proceed to the one about you not calling since. Then we can—"

He held up his hand. "Okay. Those two are the big ones. Let's save the rest for later."

She waited, clearly enjoying the hell out of watching him suffer. That was okay. He deserved that.

"I haven't contacted you because I felt I was pushing you on Saturday. I do that sometimes. You didn't want to go with me that night, but I wouldn't let you say no."

He heard her toe tapping the other side of the door. "Okay," she said. "See you around." She attempted to close the door.

He barely managed to get the heel of his hand in the door before she could shut it. "Hey. I wasn't finished."

"I think you were."

"I wasn't. On Saturday night, even before then, I thought we were getting close. I like being with you. You must know that—I'm not a subtle guy. We have a history, and I don't expect you to get over that just because I buy a bottle of cheap wine and crank up country music on the CD player."

The door opened a couple of inches. He managed to glimpse the roses in her wallpaper. "Jenna, I don't want to stop seeing you. And I'll take my lead from you. If you want to be friends, I'm fine with that. If you want to see where this relationship goes, I'm right there with you."

All he wanted to do was push the damn door open, take her in his arms and kiss her dizzy.

He flattened his hand on the door. "Can I come in?"

She sighed. "It's getting late."

"Not in California. It's only a little after six out there." He held up the envelope he'd brought. "And besides, I have something to show you."

She stared at it. "What's in there?"

"Pictures of the lighthouse. You haven't been there for a while and I thought you'd like to see what it looks like today. I hired a guy to help me paint the outside. He's a professional, so it doesn't look like graffiti gone bad."

She ran her tongue over her bottom lip and drew the door open wide.

JENNA STEPPED BACK to let Nate in. She immediately regretted it, after breathing in the subtle scent of spice in his aftershave. Taking in the way his hair fell onto his forehead, his piercing blue eyes.

He opened the envelope and pulled out a stack of photos. She could offer him something, she supposed. Perhaps coffee and a slice of the Black Forest cake in the refrigerator. But that might indicate that she was inviting him to stay awhile.

"Would you like some cake?" she heard herself say.

"That would be great."

"Coffee?"

"I don't drink coffee this late. Have you got any milk?"

She went into the kitchen, cut him a big piece of cake and poured the milk. When she returned to the living room, he had settled onto her sofa.

She took a sip of her Dr. Pepper. He ate a forkful of cake and washed it down with milk. "Good!" he declared.

"My mother's secret recipe. Everyone in town

loves it. You're eating the one she made two days ago for Mr. Levinsky. Remember him?"

"Cripes. He must be a hundred years old by now."

"Ninety-eight. That's his birthday cake. He died on Tuesday and the family didn't pick up their order."

Nate stared down at the cake. "I feel like I'm robbing pennies from a dead man's eyes."

"Don't be silly. Mr. Levinsky doesn't know you're eating his cake."

"Ha! This is Finnegan Cove. I don't think anybody ever really leaves this place."

Jenna smiled. She used to feel that way about her great-grandfather, when she went to the station. That he was still there guarding the inlet. But that was before Harley killed her father and her connection to the place.

"I'd like to look at the pictures," she said.

She really was curious. He was going to try to show her proof that the place she wanted to destroy could be brought back to its former glory. Redeemed. Right.

He smiled. "I think you'll be surprised."

She studied the photos. He'd done exactly as she'd suggested. The cottage and tower were a dazzling white, reflecting the brilliance of the sun, and trimmed in black. And the door and window trim was brick-red. She flipped through the pictures, each showing the station at a different angle. In its renewed state, it didn't seem a place populated by ghosts. But Jenna still knew.

She put the photos back in the envelope. "You've

done a fine job, Nate. I'm certain your muse will move in and inspire you to great things."

He grinned. "I think she's already there. But she's taking a long time to become adjusted to her new surroundings. So far she's only inspiring me to paint."

Jenna picked up his plate and glass.

"Is this my cue to leave?" Nate asked.

"Yep."

"Okay. Thanks for…looking at the pictures."

"No problem," she called from the kitchen.

But he was still there when she came back to the living room.

"I'm not that bad boy anymore, Jenna," he said, staring out her front window.

She didn't know what to say.

He stood and came around the coffee table. Placing his hands on her shoulders, he said, "You know the biggest problem I have being a Shelton?"

She shook her head.

"We take what we want. We don't ask." He bent and brushed his lips over hers. Then he backed away, picked up the envelope and slipped it into the back pocket of his jeans. "But I'm trying to do better. Next time I'll ask first."

She clasped her hands at her waist. Next time. When would that be? Five days from now, after he disappeared again?

He stopped at the door. "Go out with me tomorrow night. I've heard about a place north of here where they serve great speckled trout."

Her hands tightened in a white-knuckled grip. He wasn't going to disappear. But she answered the way she knew she should to protect herself from getting hurt. "I can't. There's a party at Sunshine House."

"You have to be there?"

"I'm bringing the cake. And I'm calling the bingo numbers. I promised."

"Okay. Saturday."

She swallowed. "George. We always…"

"Right. George."

She didn't have a date with George. She hadn't spoken to him in days.

"Come to the station on Saturday afternoon after you get off work. I'll order a pizza and pretend I took you for a fish dinner."

"I don't know, Nate."

He opened the door. "I'm allowing myself to hope, Jenna. Is there any reason I shouldn't?"

THE NEXT AFTERNOON, Jenna arrived at Sunshine House an hour early for the annual spring fling. She left a box of decorations in the meeting area and headed down the hallway to Hester's room. Her grandmother was watching television. "Hi," Jenna said. "Am I interrupting anything?"

Hester shut off the TV. "Heavens no. I can watch this again later on the soap channel." She patted the chair beside her. "Come sit. Tell me what's going on at the lighthouse."

"I haven't been there much," Jenna said.

"But you have been there?"

"Yes. Nate's fixing it up."

"And how are you getting along with him?"

Jenna sat on the edge of the chair. "That's not important, is it?"

Hester gave her a sly look, one Jenna didn't see too often. But it convinced her that her grandmother's faculties were very much in working order. "So, Jenna, tell me. Do you still hold the Sheltons responsible for all the evil in the world?"

She rolled her eyes. "Very funny, Gran. No. I hold Harley responsible for a major one, and Nate responsible for buying the lighthouse out from under me."

Hester tsked. "My, yes. That still is a shock. And I'm sure you had great plans to fix the place up yourself."

Jenna didn't answer.

"Keep an eye on him," Hester said. "I don't want him violating the integrity of our lighthouse."

Jenna shifted in her chair. "You want me to spy on Nate?"

"Yes, indeed. Do it for me."

## CHAPTER THIRTEEN

On Saturday, Jenna left the bakery at two o'clock and drove directly to the lighthouse.

"Good. You're here," Nate said, coming out the front door. "Let's go shopping."

"Shopping?" She let herself be turned around and steered toward his pickup.

"Yep."

"I came here for pizza," she said as she slid into the passenger seat.

"I called in an order. We'll pick it up on the way out of town."

"What are we shopping for?"

"Stuff. I had a professional decorator do my place in California. I came in when it was all done and paid her. I don't think I've bought anything besides paper towels since."

"You bought your own furniture," Jenna pointed out.

"True. And basically, if a chair doesn't make my butt hurt, I'm happy with it." He started the truck and backed onto the road. "But this cottage is bland. The only artwork I have is that photo of Sean, and even you have to admit he doesn't do much to liven the place up."

"You could use some accessories," Jenna admitted.

"I knew you'd see my point. Where do you go for this kind of thing?"

"There's a Bed, Bath and Beyond about ten miles from here."

"Sounds perfect." He patted his pocket. "When we get there, I'll push the cart and you handle the credit card."

She laughed. "Those are dangerous words, mister."

He smiled. "Don't you know by now that I'm a man who likes to live on the edge?"

"I do know that," she said. "I saw you dodging planks in the tower the other day."

Two hours later they arrived back, loaded down with pictures, rugs, linens and window coverings. And a trio of caricature sailor statues carved out of wood, which were perhaps the tackiest things Jenna had ever seen. But Nate loved them. She kidded him about spending so much money for closet decorations.

By six o'clock the kitchen cupboards were filled with dishes, pots and pans, the drawers with silverware and towels. And Jenna and Nate sat at the table sharing the warmed-up pizza.

When she'd eaten her fill, she licked sauce off her finger. "Delicious."

He stood and offered his hand. "Come with me."

Jenna hesitated. "Where are we going?"

"To the top."

"Of the lighthouse?"

"You think you can manage seventy-two steps after all that pizza?"

"I can climb circles around you any day," she said. "But are you certain the stairs will support us?"

"Of course. I fixed them, remember?"

"I remember you *said* you were going to fix them."

"Trust me, Jenna."

"Trust a guy who writes screenplays to repair a century-old staircase?" She took his hand. "Lead on. I'm right behind you."

NATE HAD FORGOTTEN how good it felt to be with a woman who didn't have an ulterior motive. Or at least, if she did, Jenna's had nothing to do with how she could use him to help her career.

"Good job, Hollywood," she said when she reached the top. She crossed to one of the windows in the hexagon-shaped beacon room, a window he'd left open, and leaned on the sill. "When I was a kid, I thought I could see the whole world from up here."

She seemed as much a part of the place as the cupola above their heads and what remained of the original glass in the windows.

He stepped onto the platform where the Fresnel lens had once been. "It's a shame the light isn't here."

She waved him over to the window. "Look. There's my house. You can just see the chimney."

He leaned out beside her. "And there's Main Street and the bakery. And Sunshine House, where I understand they had a riproaring party last night."

Jenna smiled. "They did at that." She remained silent a moment, her elbows propped on the sill, her eyes squinting in the breeze off the lake, which colored her cheeks a pale pink.

Nate threaded his hands together to keep from touching her, and studied her profile.

"I'm having a hard time staying mad at you," she said quietly.

He laughed. "I consider that a triumph."

"So has she done her job yet?"

He stared at her. "She? Who do you mean?"

"Your muse." Jenna looked down at the panorama below. "I would think this place would offer enough inspiration for even the worst writer's block."

"Maybe." He believed he was with his muse now. But as close as he felt to Jenna, secrets still kept them apart.

He stayed silent for two reasons—the promise he'd made his father, who was protecting the woman he loved. And Nate's own reluctance to spoil what was happening between him and Jenna. He hadn't felt this connected with another person in a long time.

As if reading his mind, she said, "I hope the person you're fixing the station for appreciates what you've done." She stared out at the sun, which had nearly completed its descent into the lake.

He reached over and took her arm. "Jenna, I don't know what's going to happen with the lighthouse. Truly I don't. Things change. People do things that surprise us, disappoint us. Maybe the whole scheme I had in mind when I bought the place will never materialize."

He looked into her eyes. Being here just felt so right. "Working on the lighthouse, being with you…I'll never forget it." He leaned forward, wrapped his hand around the nape of her neck and drew her close for a gentle kiss, as they stood in the last warm rays of the sun.

When he lifted his head, she stepped back and sighed. He wrapped his arm around her waist. Breathing into her ear, he said, "Call George. Tell him you have plans for tonight."

She backed farther away, struggling to regain her emotional equilibrium. "George." She wriggled free of Nate's hold and bolted for the stairs.

"Wait."

"I can't. It's late," she lied. "I forgot about my date."

She was a full story below him when he reached the top step. "This isn't having the effect I was hoping for when I brought up his name."

Jenna stopped long enough to shoot a glance over her shoulder. "What did you think would happen?"

"I hoped you might say, 'George who?'"

She reached the ground level about a half-dozen heartbeats before he did. He caught up to her in the kitchen and grabbed her by the wrist. "So this is it? You're leaving?"

"I can't break my date."

He took a deep breath, wrapped his hands around her head and plastered her lips with kisses. "Just my luck," he said, his mouth hovering above hers. "Of all the women in the world, I've got to be half-crazy about one who thinks it's important to keep her word."

"Why would you be interested in someone who didn't believe that?"

He dropped his hands. "You're right. Go."

She yanked her keys out of her pocket and headed for the door, saying over her shoulder as she went, "Did you say 'half-crazy'?"

He blinked. "Yeah, I guess I did."

"Interesting." She closed the door behind her. A moment later, she checked her smile in the rearview mirror of her car. It was positively dazzling.

NATE SANK ONTO THE SOFA, put his head in his hands and waited for his heart to quit racing and other working parts to accept that a lonely evening stretched ahead of him. Finally, he took a deep breath, stood and went to the window.

Before Jenna had rushed out of the lighthouse, Nate had been pretty sure they would end up in that brand-new queen-size bed. Hell, before he went to her house on Thursday, he'd stopped at the drugstore to make sure he was prepared, just in case. He wanted her. And he wanted her badly. He couldn't wait to turn into a reality every thought he'd had in the last week about kissing her, touching her, making love to her.

He went into the kitchen, picked up the pizza box and carried it to the trash can.

"No more secrets," he said aloud. He would go to Marion the next day. She had to tell Jenna *now*. And then he'd tell Jenna about the plans for the lighthouse. After that, maybe he could make love to her with a clear conscience. If she'd even speak to him.

It was a good scheme. And it might have worked. But there was a knock on the lighthouse door at nine o'clock. Nate got up from the sofa, where he'd been mindlessly watching TV, and opened the door to see Jenna on the threshold. She was beautiful—the most beautiful woman he'd ever laid eyes on. And she blew his good intentions all to hell.


JENNA WAITED FOR NATE to say something. He didn't; he just stared. First at her daring neckline. She'd carefully chosen a thin gold chain with a filigreed heart pendant that hung between her breasts. His gaze moved down her bare arms to her legs, pausing when he saw her sexy sandals.

"Nate?" She pulled his attention back to her face.

He cleared his throat. "You're wearing a dress."

"Yes, I am. I own a couple of dresses."

His brow furrowed. "I like this one even though you wore it for George."

*You idiot. I wore it for you.* "Well, it seemed appropriate."

The wrinkle between Nate's eyes threatened to become permanent. "So, what are you doing here?"

She smiled. "See how easily that phrase comes to mind when someone shows up, uninvited, at your house? Can I come in?"

He stepped aside to let her pass. "The funny thing is, I don't care why you're here. Any excuse works for me."

She walked into the living room. "I do have a reason."

"Am I going to like it?"

*Oh, I hope so.* "You might." She sat on the sofa, trying to appear casual, though her heart was about to jump out of her chest. She wasn't good at seduction.

She ran her tongue over her lips, which had gone dry the moment she saw Nate. He looked charmingly mussed and gorgeous in an abs-hugging T-shirt.

He sat beside her, stretching his arm over the back of the sofa. If she'd unnerved him a moment ago when she showed up, he'd regained control now. He smiled. "Should I assume the date didn't go well?"

"You can assume anything you like."

"Okay, I will." He reached for a strand of her hair and twirled the loose curl around his finger. "I like your hair this way," he said.

"Thanks."

"Can I get you something? A soda? A beer?"

"I'm fine."

He dropped his hand to her shoulder. His palm was warm on her cool skin, and he stroked down her arm. He was watching her face, and Jenna could feel her cheeks flush. If she'd been standing, she was quite sure she would have crumpled to the floor.

He turned on the sofa, cradled her cheek in his hand and kissed her. "That George is a lucky man," he said when he pulled away. "He gets to kiss you whenever he wants." Nate stood, bringing her up with him. They faced each other, close enough that their breath mingled. And then he kissed her again.

She responded with a passion that heated her blood and left them both panting.

Finally, he grasped her shoulders and looked at her with eyes that held both a question and a promise. She doubted any word but yes could come from her lips, no matter what he asked. "Jenna, is this going to happen between us?"

"Yes," she said.

"Are you sure it's what you want?"

She swallowed, nodded.

"I don't want you to think I'm rushing this."

She smiled up at him, amused by his sudden selfless attitude. "I'm thirty-three years old, Nate, and in all my life no one's ever accused me of not knowing my own mind. I'm tired of trying to hate you. It's not working."

"You don't hate me." He grinned. "I knew it."

"Don't gloat."

"Deal." He scooped her up in his arms and carried her to the bedroom. When he set her on her feet beside the bed, he removed her clothing piece by piece while she watched his slow, deliberate actions through a haze. Everywhere clothing had covered her body, he explored with his hands, making her skin tingle, bringing her alive. When she was naked, he pulled the bedspread back and laid her down with a kiss. After quickly undressing, he opened the night-stand drawer, removed a square foil package and tore the end.

"You knew I was going to show up tonight?"

He joined her on the bed and covered her face with light, moist kisses. "It wasn't premonition, Jenna. I'd rather call it preparing for a miracle."

"I can't believe this…with you," she murmured. *After all these years…*

His expression sobered. His hands stopped gently caressing her temples and he said, "We don't have to do this. If you don't think the time is right… If there's something we need to talk about first…"

She put her hand over his. "Be quiet, Nate. Haven't we talked enough?"

# CHAPTER FOURTEEN

At NINE-THIRTY SUNDAY morning, Nate drove down the narrow street of modest bungalows and looked for the one belonging to Marion. Spotting her Ford in the driveway of a frame home with cream-colored siding, he pulled in and steeled himself for a confrontation. After last night he refused to wait any longer.

He strode up her front walk and knocked. Marion came to the door wearing a housecoat and slippers. But her hair was neatly combed and she'd applied some makeup. This was Sunday. She had plans.

Her eyes rounded. "Nate? What's going on?"

He entered when she pulled the door back and turned to face her. "This is it, Marion. Game over."

"What are you talking about?"

"I think you know. Today's the day. You're telling Jenna about you and my father. She'll probably figure out then why I bought the lighthouse, but I'll try to explain to her why I didn't tell her the truth before now." He made a show of checking his wristwatch. "I'm seeing her at one o'clock. Pre-arranged. That gives you a little over three hours."

Jenna's mother twisted a dish towel in her hands. "I can't do this according to your schedule, Nate."

"For God's sake, Marion, my father is being released a week from Friday. That's less than two weeks from now. You don't have the luxury of waiting any longer."

"I have plans for this morning. And I can't just spring this on her."

"Change them," he said. "And then tell her. You have until one o'clock."

"I resent this ultimatum, Nate." Her voice shook. "You act as though I'm trying to avoid my responsibility."

He scowled. "No kidding?"

Marion pressed her lips together. "Stop looking at me like that! I love my daughter! I only want to spare her pain."

"Believe it or not, Marion, I have some experience with those same emotions myself."

Her eyes widened.

"And you and I are not sparing her pain by lying to her." He tapped his watch. "Three hours." He turned and walked out the door.

JENNA HIT THE Print button on her computer after typing the last entry into her bibliography. As the machine spat out the printed copy, she squared the loose pages and fitted them into a binder. She'd finished her night class assignment, "Herbal Remedies for Advanced Memory Loss." Thankfully, she'd had only a few final touches to make this morning. After last night, she didn't think she could concentrate on details.

Checking the clock, Jenna put the kettle on for another cup of tea. It was ten-thirty. She had two and a half hours before she'd agreed to meet Nate at the lighthouse. They were finally going for that trout dinner.

The phone rang as the kettle whistled. Marion's name showed on the caller ID. "Hi, Mom."

"Jenna, could you come over here?"

"Can it wait, Mom? I have plans for this afternoon, and I have to shower and dress."

"No, honey. This can't."

"Why don't you tell me what this is about over the phone?"

"I need to see you."

Jenna frowned. What could be so important? She reconsidered quickly. If she hurried, she could squeeze in a visit. "Okay. I'll come on over."

"I'm here, Mom," Jenna called a short time later as she walked through the front door.

"I'll be out in a minute," her mom said from the kitchen. "I'm fixing us brunch. Nothing fancy. Just eggs and sausage."

Jenna smiled to herself. She'd have to eat lightly so she wouldn't spoil her appetite. She set her purse on the credenza next to Saturday's stack of mail. It occurred to her that she hadn't checked her own mailbox yesterday. Her mind had been preoccupied.

She absently flipped through the envelopes. A letter near the bottom of the stack caught her attention and she slid it out. The return address blurred before her eyes and she blinked hard, bringing it back into focus. Her mother had gotten mail from Michigan's Department of Corrections.

The envelope was open. *Oh, my God. This is why Mom wanted to see me. This must be news about Harley.*

Jenna regretted not having checked her own mail. At least she could have been prepared. She took the letter out. "How long you going to be, Mom?" she called into the kitchen.

"A few minutes. I've put the biscuits in the oven. Make yourself comfortable."

Jenna unfolded the letter. The top of the page identified Harley Shelton's case number. There were dates listed, including those of the trial and sentencing hearing. What followed was legalese regarding a statute pertaining to victims' rights, and a notification statement of some sort.

As Jenna skimmed the letter, her attention was captured by one phrase: "…pertaining to the upcoming release of Harley Shelton." It couldn't be. Harley had been sentenced to twenty-four years. His status as a prisoner hadn't changed. She leaned against the credenza and kept reading. "…granting of parole effective May 23…It is the obligation of the Department of Corrections to inform you of the release date…."

She dropped the letter to the floor and pressed her hand to her stomach, fighting a wave nausea. Harley Shelton was being released in less than two weeks! Why hadn't her mom been told before this? She would have objected. Two weeks wasn't nearly enough time to prepare.

She pictured her mother in the kitchen, trying to find a way to soften the news. Placing Jenna's needs above her own.

And then Jenna's knees went weak. Nate knew it! That's why he'd come back. That's why he was living in the lighthouse—to be near when his father was set free. Jenna moved to the sofa and sat heavily.

She bit her lips to keep them from trembling. The pain kept her mind sharp. She needed to be strong to help her mother. But then another realization hit her, and she felt as if she were a fragile leaf being buffeted in the wind. The lighthouse. Nate wasn't just living there. He'd bought it to… No. Nate wouldn't have bought the lighthouse for his father. Harley couldn't be the person he'd spoken about so vaguely…

Jenna struggled with the overwhelming evidence. Harley wouldn't want to return to Finnegan Cove. He was hated by everyone who knew Joseph Malloy. He would want to move as far away from this town as he could, so he wouldn't have to face her and her mother. And no way would he want to live in the very place where the tragedy had occurred. There must be an explanation.

From what seemed a great distance away, Jenna heard her mother's voice. "It's ready. Come into the kitchen…"

Jenna looked up. Her mother gasped as she saw the letter lying on the floor. "Oh, Jenna, you saw it." Her words rushed out on a trembling breath of air. "I wanted to tell you."

Jenna stood up and reached for her hand. "Mom, I'm so sorry. Do you know why the state granted Harley parole? Can this be overturned? Isn't there something we can do?"

Marion closed her other hand over both of theirs. "Honey, you don't understand."

"I know you must be devastated. But…but it'll be okay. We'll face this together." Jenna stopped when she saw an unexpected look pass over her mother's face. Not anger. Not determination. It was regret and guilt. Marion grasped Jenna's hands until it hurt and began sobbing.

"There's something you don't know."

"I do know, Mom," she said. "And it's all right. Nate must have purchased the lighthouse for his father. I can't believe he would do something like that. He has to know that we won't welcome Harley back."

*He has to know that after last night, he's breaking my heart.*

Blinking away her tears, Marion took a shaky breath, but held on to Jenna's hand. "Sweetheart, there's so much you don't understand. When you think about it, you'll see that the lighthouse is the perfect place for Harley."

Jenna stared at her mother. "Who cares what's perfect for Harley? He's a murderer."

"Oh, honey…"

Jenna gripped Marion's shoulders. "You don't have to be strong in front of me, Mom. You don't have to pretend. I know this must be killing you."

Marion straightened her back. "Is that true, Jenna? I don't have to pretend with you?"

"Of course not. I know how you feel."

"No, honey, you don't." She took a deep breath. "The truth is, I *want* Harley to come back."

Jenna dropped her hands to her sides. "Mom, you think that's what you want now. You need revenge. You think you can make Harley's life a living hell here. You think you'll remind him every day of what he did to our family. But it won't work. You've always told me to move on—"

"Jenna, stop it!" Marion's voice broke. Her expression nearly ripped Jenna's heart in two. "I want Harley back because I'm in love with him."

Jenna cringed, suddenly feeling small and weak. She had to have heard wrong. Love? They'd always hated Harley. It was the bond that had gotten them through the death—the murder—of her dad. She took several steps back. "No, Mom, you don't mean it. You're confused."

"No, Jenna, I'm not. I do love Harley. I've loved him for years, since before—"

Jenna thrust her hand in front of her eyes, blocking the image of her mother's face. "Don't say another word. You're talking crazy. You can't love Harley. He's been in prison for twenty years! He killed your husband, my father!"

"I'm sorry, sweetheart, but Harley didn't mean to kill Joseph." She gulped a breath. "I was there. I saw it all."

"You were there?" Jenna's shock was giving way to anger. "No, *I* was there. Remember? I saw the gash in Dad's head. I saw the blood on the floor and on Harley's hands. I smelled it! I didn't see you."

Marion looked at the floor. Tears dripped onto her blouse. "I know. I ran." She gulped again. "I didn't know you were in the truck."

Jenna's mind spun. For a moment she thought she might faint. She bit her lip, drawing blood. The sour metallic taste jerked her into startled awareness. "You saw it happen? And now you say Harley didn't mean it? Harley didn't pick up that two-by-four?" Jenna took her mother by the arms and shook her. "Is that right, Mom? Harley didn't slam Daddy in the head with that board?"

Marion refused to look at Jenna. Her silence answered the question.

"Did Daddy have a weapon?" Jenna asked. "Did he threaten Harley?"

Marion shook her head. She began to sob loudly.

Jenna started to laugh, an eerie sound. "And yet you say that the man who picked up a board and slammed it into an unarmed human being didn't *mean it?*" She stared out the window at her mother's walk, which was lined with amber marigolds. "Mom, what's happened to you?"

Tears streaked Marion's cheeks. "Jenna, he never meant…"

"You've all conspired against me." Jenna's voice was hoarse. She pushed the words out through the terrible constriction that had gripped her throat. "And you, Mom, you've lied to me for years."

"If you'll just sit down and give me a chance…"

Confusion and bitterness threatened to consume Jenna. "If Harley Shelton comes back to Finnegan Cove, I'm leaving. I'll take Gran with me, and I'll never return."

She slammed her mother's door behind her.

## CHAPTER FIFTEEN

JENNA COULDN'T go home and knew she shouldn't drive. Her heart was pounding furiously, each beat reverberating in her head. She would never forgive her mother. She would never forgive Nate, but she'd be damned if she'd let either one of them cause her to die of a stroke, alone in her car. She pointed her Jeep toward Big Bear River and Valerie's condo. When she saw her friend's car in the driveway, she began to cry.

Valerie answered the door when she rang the bell, took one look at Jenna's face and opened her arms. Jenna cried for half an hour, and somehow the story made it through her hiccups and sobbing.

After drinking the tea laced with bourbon her friend made for her, Jenna was calm enough to think rationally. Sort of.

"What are you going to do?" Valerie asked.

"Hide for a while. Never speak to any of them."

She nodded. "Okay. It's a plan, at least. You going to tell Hester?"

Jenna rolled her head, loosening the tense

muscles in her neck. "Oh, jeez. Gran. It won't be easy, but I'll have to. I can't count on my mother to tell the truth."

"Hester might already know," Valerie suggested. "She's spooky. It's like she's got these antennae and she never misses anything."

"She doesn't have any idea about this. Mom and Harley? I guarantee if she did, she'd have done something to stop it."

Valerie shrugged. "Some things are unstoppable, love being one of them."

"Love!" Jenna spat the word. "You know, George was right. He said Nate wasn't to be trusted. He called him slick." She blew out a breath. "Boy, was he right."

"Does this mean you're going back to George now?"

Jenna thought a moment. "No. Something honest at least came of this mess. I was forced to examine my feelings for George." She sighed. "George is better off without me."

"So what's the plan for today?" Valerie asked. "Do we head over to the Texaco, fill up a gas can and torch the lighthouse?"

Jenna must have teared up, because her friend quickly said, "I'm kidding."

"We can't stay here," Jenna stated. "It's almost one o'clock, the time I'd promised to meet Nate." She snorted. "It would be just like him to start looking for me."

Valerie picked up the empty teacups. "He does have a lot to feel guilty about. But you know, he never did really lie."

Jenna glared sharply at her. "What?"

"I'm just saying…all he ever did was give you some crap about having 'his reasons' for buying the lighthouse. Maybe he'd promised not to say. And that stuff about him hoping to get past writer's block might have been true."

"Are you defending him?"

"No. I'm on your side, all the way. I just think that in all fairness—"

"Fairness? Do you honestly think anyone has been *fair* with me? And now I have to leave town before that murdering bastard moves back in!"

Valerie carried the cups into her kitchen. When she returned, her expression was thoughtful. "You said Marion admitted that her relationship with Harley began before the murder?"

Jenna nodded. "Can you believe it?"

"No, actually." Valerie sat. "Your mom doesn't seem like the type to cheat on her husband. I wonder what she saw in Harley? And what she didn't see in Joseph?"

Jenna scoffed. "I suppose she didn't care for hard-working, loyal men. She preferred roughneck drunks." Jenna waited for Valerie to react, but her friend remained expressionless. "What are you thinking?"

"Nothing. It's just weird, that's all."

Jenna didn't like the direction Valerie's observation was leading. She didn't want to entertain any thoughts that her father had been less than the perfect man she'd always believed him to be.

JENNA TURNED ONTO her street after ten that night. Once she'd left Valerie's, she'd driven around awhile, thinking, trying not to feel sorry for herself. She'd never forgive Nate for making her love him. Why hadn't she followed her instincts about him? Why had she allowed his charm to sway her? And why, in heaven's name, had she desired him beyond all reason? She'd wanted Nate with a passion she'd never known before. And while she couldn't forgive him, she couldn't forgive herself, either.

She parked in her driveway and got out of the Jeep. She was halfway to the door when a truck pulled in behind her car. The headlights instantly dimmed and Nate got out. She almost had her key in the lock when he yanked it from her hand.

"Where the hell have you been?" he demanded.

She'd had lots of time to think about what she would do when she saw him again. Now, as he stood scowling down at her, all she could do was will her tears not to fall.

She swallowed. "Go away."

"Jenna, I…" His voice softened. "I know you found out. I know you must hate all of us. But we've been worried sick about you. I've been calling you all day."

She'd turned off her cell phone after three calls had come in while she drove to Valerie's. "I even went to your friend's place, but she wasn't home. Where were you?"

Jenna grabbed for her keys, but he gripped them tighter. "Where I go is none of your business."

He combed his fingers through his hair. "I should have told you everything."

She took a quick, fortifying breath. "Ya think, Nate?"

He reached for her, but she jerked away. "Jenna, I'm sorry. I hated not telling you…"

She narrowed her eyes.

He raised his hand. "Okay, maybe I didn't hate it at first, when I met you again and you jumped to conclusions about me."

"Conclusions that were proved correct."

"Damn it, Jenna, I'm not my father! I wanted to tell you everything once I realized that…"

"Realized what, Nate? That you could hurt me? That I was starting to care about you?"

"Partly. But mostly I wanted to tell you when I realized that *I* had feelings *for you*. Give me a chance to explain, to tell you about my dad, to make this all up to you."

"I know all I need to know about Harley." She straightened her spine. "I told you to leave. Now."

After a few tense moments, he said, "This isn't over, Jenna."

She held out her hand and wiggled her fingers,

waiting until he dropped the keys into her palm, then went inside and slammed the door in his face. She felt a little better. As if maybe after she'd cried for a few more hours she might be able to sleep.

VALERIE FILLED Jenna's wineglass for the second time and sat back on the wrought-iron bench in Jenna's backyard.

"You trying to get me drunk?" Jenna asked. "It's okay if you are."

Valerie chuckled. "Can't hurt and it might help."

Jenna took a sip. "I'm sorry I'm such lousy company."

"You're not." Valerie glanced at the flowers beginning to bloom in Jenna's backyard. "I can't think of anything I'd rather do on a gorgeous Saturday afternoon than let you pay me back for the number of times I've depended on you to get me out of a funk. But I don't think my rotten moods lasted this long."

Jenna grimaced. "It's only been a week. I'm just getting started."

"So how's it working out for you?"

Jenna sipped more wine. "It's beginning to cheer me up. At least I've had the pleasure of ignoring Nate all three times he's come into the bakery this week."

"You go, girl. It feels great to give someone the cold shoulder, doesn't it?"

She nodded.

"I do feel somewhat responsible for this mess," Valerie said. "I'm the one who suggested the possibilities between you and him in the first place."

Jenna swirled the liquid in her glass.

"You really should talk to him, Jen," Valerie said. "The guy deserves a chance to explain his hideously insensitive treatment of you. Especially since you've been nothing but sugar and spice to him since he got to town."

"I can't talk to him. Have you forgotten? I slept with him. Worse, I threw myself at him."

"So you slept with him. Big deal. How many guys have you slept with who ended up disappointing you?"

Jenna could only stare at her best friend.

Valerie responded with a self-deprecating laugh. "Oh, right. That's me. I'm the one who has the long list of throwaway sexual partners. You're the one whose list is so short you remember every name, address and size of their boxers."

"It's not just that he disappointed me. It's not like he decided he couldn't marry a woman with my haircut. He made me think he could love me. He made me think I could love him."

Valerie's eyes widened. "Marriage? You were thinking about marrying Nate?"

"No, of course not. He lives in California, for heaven's sake." She took another sip of wine. "Well, maybe it crossed my mind." Hmm. The wine seemed to be acting like truth serum.

"I don't want to play devil's advocate, Jen, because Nate should have told you he bought the lighthouse for his father. But I think he *would* have told you. He was waiting for your mom. This thing between her and Harley was her secret."

Jenna snorted. "What does that even mean? My mother waited twenty years to tell me the truth. And then told me only because Harley was about to show up on Main Street."

"And I've apologized, Jenna, over and over again."

Both women turned to stare at Marion, who had come in the gate. She had a baking dish in her hands.

"Hi, Mrs. M.," Valerie said. "Join the party. Especially if you've brought food."

Jenna looked down at her glass.

"Lasagna," Marion said. "I owe Jenna a meal. She didn't stay for brunch last Sunday."

After an uncomfortable silence, Valerie nudged Jenna. "Where are your manners? Invite your mom to go into the kitchen and get plates."

Jenna rolled her eyes. She'd hadn't been able to avoid her mother, since they both worked at the bakery. But she wouldn't ever forgive her. "You can stay, Mom. The lasagna smells great, and obviously Valerie will blame me forever if she doesn't get some."

"That's my girl," Valerie said. "Way to roll out that red carpet."

A few minutes later Marion had served up three healthy portions of pasta. Then she poured herself a glass of wine. "So what are we talking about?" she asked. "Nate Shelton?"

Valerie chuckled. "Is there another topic worth discussing?"

"Well, we could discuss George Lockley." Marion darted a quick glance at her daughter. "What's going on with you and George?"

Jenna stared at the maple tree at the edge of her property. "This girl-talk isn't going to work, Mom."

Marion looked at Valerie.

"They broke up," Valerie said.

"Oh."

"My friend decided that George was a bit too tame for her. She much prefers the roller-coaster ride of true love." When Jenna glared at her, she added, "Someday she'll know I'm right about this."

Marion smiled reflectively. "I think I know something about that myself." She set down her plate. "Which brings me to the real reason I'm here."

The other two stopped eating.

"Jenna, I spoke with Harley today. In fact, I've talked to him nearly every day since Sunday."

Jenna tapped her fork on the side of her plate. "How nice for you."

Undaunted, Marion continued. "Harley and I discussed you."

"How nice for me."

"We think you should come with me when I visit him tomorrow. It's the last chance you'll have to speak with him before he gets out on Friday."

Jenna dropped the fork. "I think I've been pretty clear when it comes to Harley, Mom. I hadn't planned to speak with him at all. Ever."

"I know that. But you're making a mistake."

Jenna started to get up, but Marion gripped her forearm. "I'm not going to let you run away."

Jenna frowned, but stayed where she was.

Marion drew a deep breath. "Sweetheart, sometimes people do the wrong things for what they perceive to be the right reasons. I want you to think about that before you continue to condemn Harley for the rest of your life. And I want you to think about it when you tell yourself you're through with Nate."

Jenna couldn't believe what her mother had just said. "Are you trying to say that Harley killed Daddy for the 'right reasons'?"

"Not exactly. But he had a reason, and he wants to tell you what it was. He wants to try to help you make sense of the grief you've felt since your father died."

Tears stung Jenna's eyes. She didn't want to go over this again. "There was a trial, Mom. Lawyers, a judge and a jury made sense of what happened that night."

"No, not really." Marion paused, held her glass out to Valerie. "Fill me up again." After she'd taken a long drink, she said, "They couldn't, because I was never called to testify."

Jenna stared at her mother. "No matter how you

think you feel about Harley now, you wouldn't have testified for him."

Marion swallowed, looked down. "Yes, I would have. I *should* have."

## CHAPTER SIXTEEN

MARION PICKED JENNA up at ten the next morning. They didn't speak much as they drove through a constant rain. Jenna watched the mesmerizing rhythm of the windshield wipers, trying to pretend she was going anywhere other than the Foggy Creek prison.

"It's just around the next bend," Marion said finally, glancing over at her. "We'll be the first to arrive, just ahead of regular visiting hours. It's a privilege Harley has earned over the last year or so."

Jenna began to perspire. She wiped her hands on her slacks and wondered again why she'd agreed to do this. Why she'd agreed to see the man whose accomplishment her mother had just mentioned with such pride.

Through the drizzle pooling on the windshield of Marion's car, a colorless, stone-walled monolith appeared from out of the equally nondescript landscape. Occupying several dozen grassless, mist-shrouded acres, today Foggy Creek Correctional Facility was indeed wrapped in a thick, damp fog.

Six towers projected from the hexagon of walls standing at least ten feet high. Each tower was connected to the next by a menacing coil of barbed wire. Floodlights topped each guard post.

Jenna stared at the sprawling, drab structure and clutched her stomach. For the first time, she considered that even the worst of humanity, Harley Shelton, didn't deserve this fate. And then she reminded herself what he had done.

Marion parked the car, took a plastic rain hat from her purse, put it on and tied the strings under her chin. Watching her, Jenna realized that this was Marion's life, her connection to the man she loved. She wasn't about to let her hair, which she'd carefully curled, be ruined by the rain.

She looked at Jenna. "I have an umbrella in the trunk. I'll get it for you if you want."

"That's okay. It's only sprinkling."

They got out of the car and walked to a gated entrance. The guard smiled at Marion. "I guess I won't be seeing much of you after this," he said.

It was a surreal comment. Jenna had never known about this part of her mother's life and the odd network of acquaintances Marion had developed over two decades.

The guard let them through to a set of steel doors leading to the main prison building. "You don't have anything metal in your purse, do you, Jenna?" her mom asked. "No nail file or clippers?"

Jenna made a quick check. "No, I don't think so."

Another employee, also familiar with Marion, let them in. "Normally, they ask who you've come to see," she whispered to Jenna. "But these guards already know."

Next their purses were scanned in a metal detector, and they were both frisked and checked with a body wand. They proceeded to a desk where their driver's licenses were run through a copy machine, and they filled out a visitor's record card indicating the date and time of their arrival.

Another guard hit a buzzer that opened an interior door, and they walked down a well-lit, wide hallway. The walls were gray plaster, the ceiling dingy white. The floor was covered in a pale beige linoleum worn down at the center. A faint pine scent lingered in the air, prompting Jenna to note that the entire area was spotlessly clean. It was Sunday after all, the traditional day for families to come together.

They entered a room sparsely furnished with small rectangular tables. One corner had a bookcase with a few dozen children's books and a ragged wicker basket holding a smattering of toys.

Marion took a seat at one of the tables. "Sit down, honey," she said.

"I'd rather stand." Jenna paced to the window, which provided natural light, but was too high to see out. After a few minutes, during which Jenna thought her nerve endings were going to ignite, the door opened and a man stepped inside.

Marion stood and the years faded from her face.

Jenna leaned against the wall, her hands behind her, palms pressed against the cool plaster. She barely recognized Harley Shelton. This tall, broad-shouldered man, with his thick gray hair neatly combed and his clothes clean and pressed, didn't look like a monster.

She blinked, brought his face into focus. The Harley she remembered—the man her father had accused of tangling his fishing nets, sabotaging his motors, stealing his customers—had been a gruff, hot-tempered, unkempt brute who wielded a two-by-four. This man, in contrast, was an older, heavier version of his son. His back was straight, his posture confident and his expression was wise and sad.

But could Jenna believe that the other Harley didn't still exist? That under this facade, a monster wasn't waiting for an opportunity to return?

Marion hugged him. He glanced at Jenna over her shoulder and gave her a tentative smile. Then he kissed her mom's cheek respectfully.

"Come here, Jenna," Marion said. "Sit with us and hear what Harley has to say."

She approached slowly. Harley held out his hand. Jenna put hers behind her back. "Well, look at you," he said softly. "Prettier than I remember, though I've seen lots of pictures." He dropped his hand to his side. "I'm so glad you came, Jenna. It's been so long."

She sat down woodenly, her knees aching from the simple movement. "It was important to Mom."

He sat across from both women. "I appreciate it." He gazed at Marion, his expression loving, almost reverent. "Your mother can be a stubborn woman. But most of the time, I'm glad of it."

Jenna folded her hands on the table. "So what have I come here to learn?"

Harley rubbed his thumb over his mustache. "It's time you heard what happened that night. And it's time you know how sorry I am for what I did."

At least he wasn't denying his guilt. Jenna had to respect that. She waited.

"You might remember my wife, Cheryl," he began.

"Vaguely. I was quite young when she got sick."

"She was a good person. I changed when she died," he said. "I became a man no one could love or respect—" he smiled "—or, if you ask my sons, even tolerate most days." He held up one finger, making a point. "Losing Cheryl isn't an excuse for my behavior. I know that now, and I've had plenty of psychologists in this place tell me. I'm just mentioning it because that's when it started.

"I drank too much. People knew to stay out of my way when I'd been on one of my binges. I must have been a mean cuss. I remember stumbling home with bloody knuckles more than a few times. And I know my behavior put a strain on my relationship with Mike and Nate."

He'd mentioned his sons twice now, and each time, Jenna felt a stab to her heart.

"Everyone gave up on me. I can't blame them." He looked at Marion. "But not this woman. She saw something in me worth saving, and was hell-bent to do it."

Marion smiled. "I saw the man you really were, Harley. In pain and lonely with no idea how to pull yourself out of your grief. I saw the man under the misery."

His lips twitched. He looked directly at Jenna. "I'd always respected your mother," Harley said. "But when things started going wrong in my life, and she was the only one who ever showed me a kindness, my opinion of her began to change. I think maybe I worshipped her for a while."

Marion glanced at her in turn. "I know what you're thinking, honey. That I betrayed your father. But you have to understand that things hadn't been right between your daddy and me for a long time before he died. We'd grown apart. We wanted different things out of life. We even argued about how to raise you—the one bright spot in our lives, the thing that should have held us together."

"I don't believe you, Mom," Jenna said. "We were a happy family. You and Daddy…"

"You were so young," Marion said. "You weren't even aware of the problems. We hid the truth from you."

"But I would have known."

Marion sighed. "About the only thing your father and I did as a couple at the end was put up a front for you." Her eyes misted and she took a tissue from her purse. "I knew how much you loved Joseph, so for a long time I tried to keep us together as a family."

"But you did stay together." Jenna's voice cracked. "You never left Daddy."

"That's right. But I would have eventually. I didn't love him anymore. I don't think he loved me."

Something twisted painfully in Jenna's chest. She didn't think she could bear to hear another word. Her mother had cheated on her father. If Marion thought this explanation would make everything all right between her daughter and Harley, she was so wrong. Jenna started to stand. "That's enough, Mom. So, you loved Harley. So what? It doesn't change anything."

"You have to hear us out," Marion said, her voice steely. "Harley and I arranged to meet at the light-house that night. By then we'd come to know it as our place. It was secluded, dark. The vandals had ruined it, and no one went inside much, except us. We were planning to steal a couple of hours. That's all. A couple of hours together."

Harley cleared his throat, prompting Marion to pause. "Marion and I had only been there for a short time, and while we were talking, I heard someone outside the cottage. The door opened and Joe came in."

Jenna clutched her blouse. Her father had walked in on them. He'd died witnessing his wife's betrayal. Had been killed over it.

"I don't know how he knew," Marion said. "We were so careful. We didn't want you to find out. Or Nate."

Jenna remembered the phone call that had come that night. Recalled her father's anger. He must have suspected, had someone watching. Someone who never spoke at the trial. Someone loyal to Joe who wanted Harley and Marion to pay.

"He started yelling at your mother," Harley said. "He grabbed her, called her names. She begged him to let her go."

Placing her hands flat on the table, Jenna said, "My father was a gentle man."

"Sometimes he was, honey," Marion said. "But underneath he had a terrible temper. If you'll think back, you'll remember seeing it a time or two, like when his fishing catch was disappointing, when times were tough."

"But that was just about money. Everyone loses their temper over that."

"It wasn't just money, Jenna. Joe had a right to be hurt that night, I know."

"He had no right to take his anger out on Marion," Harley interrupted. "I tried to talk to him, told him it was me he should be mad at. That I should be the one taking the brunt of his fury."

"But he didn't let me go," Marion said. "He told Harley he'd get to him when he was through with me."

Jenna leaned back in the cold hard chair and

closed her eyes. She tried not to visualize a scene that might change her perception of her father forever. "Did he hit you, Mom?"

"No, he didn't, but I believe he would have. Harley…" Her eyes brimmed with tears. Marion stared at him. "Harley stopped him."

"I didn't mean to kill him, Jenna. I only meant to protect your mother. And I've been sorry for how it turned out ever since the day it happened."

"You could have stopped him with your hands," Jenna said. "You didn't have to pick up a weapon."

"You're right. But it happened so fast. I didn't think. And I've been sorry ever since."

"Sorry you didn't get what you wanted," Jenna said.

"Yes, I was sorry that I wouldn't get to make a life with Marion. Sorry that I faced losing a big chunk of what time I had left on earth. Sorry for the way I'd alienated one son and was leaving the other one who'd stayed with me. And, whether or not you believe it, sorry that I took a man's life."

Jenna let out a trembling breath. "Why didn't you tell this story in court? Why didn't you say that you were protecting my mother?"

"I tried to get him to do that," Marion said, smiling sadly. "But Harley can be stubborn, too. He told me to run that night, Jenna. He wanted me out of there before the police came." She dabbed at her eyes. "And, God forgive me, I did. I rushed out the back door and ran through the woods until I got to the main road where I'd left my car."

"Marion, the truth is I did kill Joe in a fit of rage. That's the hard fact. The whole town knew there'd been bitter feelings between us for years." He paused, shook his head. "And we don't know for sure that he would have hurt you. I've questioned my motive that night all this time, but I've never second-guessed telling you to run. You had Jenna to think about, your reputation in a town that can be unforgiving."

He wore a pained expression. Jenna dropped her head in her hands, her thoughts tumbling wildly.

"I'm sorry, Jenna, for what you saw that night," Marion said. "If I had known you were there, I wouldn't have run. But there's something else."

Jenna shut her eyes. She didn't know if she had the strength to hear more about that night.

"Harley gave me the money to buy the bakery."

She opened her eyes, stared at her mother. "What? I thought that came from Daddy's insurance."

"He didn't have any insurance, Jenna. He didn't have anything. I had enough money in the checking account when your father died to maybe live another two weeks. Then I didn't know what I would do."

Jenna stared at Harley. "That much money? How?"

"Selling his fishing boat," Marion answered for him. She gazed at Harley with such fondness that Jenna had to look away. "He told me to tell you it came from Joe, that he'd provided for us."

Jenna stood and paced. "I had no idea. I have to think."

"I know," Marion said. "You take all the time you need to sort it out."

"You mean all the time I need until Friday."

"Well…"

Jenna stood across the table from Harley. "There's still one thing…"

"Anything. Just ask."

"Why did you have Nate buy the lighthouse?"

Marion looked up at her. "I asked Harley to persuade Nate to buy the station."

"*You* asked him?"

"Yes. At first I thought Harley would just move into my house. But he refused. He said it would be enough for the town to adjust to him being back, without adding a morality issue." She actually blushed. "He wants us to be married first."

"And yet you and Harley believe he should return to the one place in the world where he isn't wanted?" she said. "To the exact place where the crime happened? And Nate went along with that? Mom, that's just a little crazy."

"That station represents the happiest times I've ever known, Jenna. I lived there as a child before my father died." She looked at Harley and her voice softened to a whisper. "The nights when we were together… I want that lighthouse for Harley and me, Jenna. I've never wanted you to tear it down. If that's selfish, then I'm sorry, but I've waited twenty years…." Her words dissolved into tears.

Harley stood and walked around the table to

Jenna. He raised his hand as if he would touch her, but then dropped it. "I don't have to live in the lighthouse, Jenna. I can make other plans."

She only shook her head. She didn't know what to think any more.

"You've heard it all," he said. "That's it. I love your mother. I will do my damnedest to take care of her the rest of my days. I know it's likely that you won't ever find room in your heart for me—" he patted his chest "—but you've always taken up a big part of mine."

She sniffed, an attempt to stop the tears that burned her eyes. "I'm not sure, Harley. I feel like I don't even know you."

"You don't. Yet."

"Did Nate know all this?"

"He found out a couple of weeks after he got to Finnegan Cove. He was as shocked as you are, and he's been hounding both of us to tell you the truth. Now it's done, and hopefully, Nate will let up on me."

Jenna's mind traveled back to that night in the woods. Nate had avoided her the next day, as if what they'd done had meant nothing to him, when it had meant everything to her. Maybe he'd found out about his father and Marion right after that. Maybe he'd been as blindsided and confused as she was now.

"He cares a whole lot for you, Jenna," Harley said. "I don't know what you're going to do with that information, and coming from me, you may not give it much credence, but you ought to know."

Marion stood and came around the table. "I'm going to take my daughter home now. I think she's had enough of us for one day."

Harley pressed his palm to her cheek. "I'm sure she has."

"I'll see you Friday at nine."

He looked around the cold, gray room. "I'll be waiting."

Jenna walked past him. She didn't speak. She didn't think she could force any more words out. Not when so many questions remained. Like how had she not known that her father, the man she adored, had had a dark side? And how had she not seen her mother's struggles to hide the truth—then and over the past many years? But in spite of what she'd faced the past half hour and all she would have to sort out in the future, Jenna felt the hole that had been in her heart for so long begin to fill up.

## CHAPTER SEVENTEEN

ON WEDNESDAY at eight-thirty, Bill Hastings walked into the bakery. "I wonder what he wants?" Jenna said, knowing the mayor usually sent his secretary to pick up his morning doughnuts.

"I expect we'll find out," Marion said. "I hope he's not here about Harley."

Marion had confided that she'd let a few people know Harley was returning. Jenna figured half the town must know by now, including the mayor.

She went to the counter, hoping to spare her mother any embarrassment if he should bring up the subject. "What can I do for you, Bill? Boston cream or chocolate covered?"

"I didn't come here for doughnuts," he said, and then peered into the display case. "But now that you mention it, I'll have one of each."

She quickly stuffed them in a bag. "That'll be one dollar and fifty-eight cents."

He set an official-looking folder on the counter and dug into his pocket. Once he'd paid, he slid the file toward her. "This is for you."

"What is it?"

"It's from the Michigan Beacon Society. Nate Shelton dropped it off yesterday so I could look at it. Then he asked me to give it to you. Said it had some information you might be interested in sometime in the future."

Jenna flipped the folder open. It contained, among general information about lighthouse conservancy, a pamphlet on how to form a nonprofit organization.

Bill stuffed half a doughnut into his mouth and headed for the door. He stopped before going out. "By the way, Marion," he mumbled, his mouth still full, "I hear Harley is being paroled in a couple of days. Nate says he'll be living in the lighthouse for a while."

Jenna looked at her mom and held her breath.

"That's right," Marion said.

Bill gave her a knowing smile. "Strange, isn't it? Harley coming back here? Things have a funny way of working themselves out, don't they, Marion?"

She remained silent.

"I don't have a problem with that," Bill said. "The man's served his time. I just think folks might wonder how you two women figure he's paid his debt to you."

Jenna leaned over the counter. "You know, Bill, you can be a big help to us by spreading the word."

He gave her a puzzled look. "What word is that?"

"If people know that Mom and I can forgive Harley, no one else in this town should have a problem giving him a chance."

"You might be right." He opened the door. "Good morning, ladies."

When he left, Marion wrapped her arms around Jenna. "Thanks for that, honey."

"Don't thank me yet, Mom. I still haven't decided how I feel about Harley."

THREE GENERATIONS OF Sean O'Hanlon's descendants shared a calorie-laden tray of desserts at the Finnegan Cove Grill where they'd gone for the all-you-can-eat Wednesday night buffet. Hester licked chocolate frosting off her fingertip, stared intently at her daughter and said, "So, you and Harley Shelton?"

"That's right. I should have told you long before this." Marion looked at Jenna. "But I made a lot of mistakes that seemed to be the right decisions at the time."

"Actually, Marion," Hester said, "you've given me a reason to live another ten years."

Marion chuckled. "How's that, Mother?"

"It will take Harley that long to prove himself to me, and I intend to stick around until he does." She took a sip of coffee. "Though I must admit I never cared much for Joe."

Jenna gasped. "Gran!"

"Sorry, dear, but Joe was a rigid man. No fun in him." She slid her spoon into her banana pudding. "Still, he didn't deserve his fate."

"No, he didn't," Jenna said.

"Now, Nathaniel, he's another story," Hester said.

"Nate doesn't have to prove himself to you?"

"He already did."

"By saving the lighthouse?" Jenna asked.

Hester only raised her eyebrows and looked over her glasses. "Among other things."

From the moment Marion and Jenna had told Hester about Nate's work at the station and Harley's plans to live there, their eerily perceptive relative had accepted the news with a shrug of contentment as if she weren't surprised at all. Jenna thought now of Valerie's reference to Hester's special antennae. "You're taking all this with amazing good grace, Gran," she said.

"I'm adaptable, Jenna. Whatever you two girls decide to do with your lives is fine with me."

Jenna doubted her grandmother's sincerity but knew better than to question it. Gran was happy. Marion was happy. And Jenna was beginning to hope that some of their good vibes would spread to her.

Hester pointed her fork at Jenna. "There is a condition to what I just said."

"Oh?"

"Everything's fine with me as long as the lighthouse stands. No more messing about with history."

"Okay," Jenna agreed, marveling at how close she was to accepting that Gran was right.

Now, at nearly nine o'clock, Jenna pulled in front of the lighthouse and turned off her engine. She tapped her fingers on the steering wheel as she stared at the station. She needed to ask Nate why he'd given her the information on the Michigan Beacon Society. Jenna could only surmise that he saw possibilities for the lighthouse that didn't include him or his dad as the owner.

Jenna had begun to consider that maybe tearing the place down would have been a mistake.

She stared at the structure she'd once loved, and found she could look at it again without the painful memories. She saw a soft glow in the parlor window, making the lighthouse appear cozy and warm. The fixture over the front door blazed a welcome and illuminated the cast-iron address numbers Nate had attached near the new brass mailbox. A breeze ruffled the lacy curtains she and Nate had recently purchased.

She got out of the Jeep and walked slowly to the small porch. Jenna raised the bar on the shiny new door knocker, but paused when a sound coming from the open window caught her attention. It was a gentle, muffled tapping, quick, steady and entirely familiar to anyone who spent hours at the computer. She could picture Nate's fingers flying over the keyboard.

She rapped lightly on the door, and the tapping stopped.

"Just leave the pizza on the stoop," Nate called out. "Your money's in the mailbox."

The sound resumed, and Jenna realized that he was obviously in some sort of writer's zone and wanted to be left alone. She spoke loudly enough to be heard, but not enough to startle him. "It's Jenna, Nate, not your pizza. But that's okay. I'll come back tomorrow."

She'd only gone a few steps when she heard the door open. The next she knew, Nate had grabbed her by the elbow and spun her around.

"Jenna!" His blue eyes were wide and a smile pulled at his lips. "Don't go."

"Are you sure? I know you're busy."

"Not too busy for you." He nodded toward the open door. "You'll come in, won't you?"

"For a few minutes. I just came to thank you for the information from the Beacon Society."

"I'm thinking it might prove helpful." He stepped aside, letting her precede him into the parlor.

She held her breath, her senses assaulted by both his presence and the bittersweet joy of being in this room again. The last time he had carried her from the parlor through—she looked toward the bedroom—that door.

"Can I get you something?" Nate said. "I have soda or wine."

"No. I'm fine." She tried to think of something else to say, but she'd already thanked him. She was done. But she certainly wasn't ready to go.

Feeling the strain of the silence, she settled her gaze on his laptop computer. "Are you working on a screenplay?"

His eyes lit with enthusiasm. "Yes. And, Jenna, it's

flowing, like the way I used to write. In the past few days, I haven't been able to get the words down fast enough."

She couldn't ignore a stab of disappointment. In the same period, she'd barely managed to keep her focus on such routine chores as filling the coffee machine and reminding herself to eat.

"Can I tell you about it?" Nate asked.

She managed a smile. "Sure."

He led her to the sofa. "Why don't you sit down." He didn't join her. His energy seemed too boundless for him to stop and sit.

"The script is called *The Redemption of Matthew Stone*." It's about a man who returns to a small lakeside town. He made some mistakes in his life, terrible ones, that almost cost him everything. But he comes out of it a stronger person for his suffering." Nate smiled. "You with me so far?"

"I think I've got the picture."

"He doesn't accomplish this transformation on his own," Nate said. "He has family who support him. And his own inner strength. It's a story that pulls at the heartstrings, but it feels like real life."

Jenna smiled. "I wonder why. I know this will be a great movie."

"But wait. Now the mind of Nate Shelton takes over. I've sort of blended two characters into one. Matthew comes back to his small town and he hooks up with a woman, a wonderful, sweet and very sexy lady who still lives there. Her name is Mary. She's honest and kind, and she disapproves of Matthew's past and his mistakes in judgment. The poor guy tries to come up with all sorts of ways to make her forgive his many faults, overlook his questionable choices and love him in spite of them."

Jenna glanced down at her lap. "I wonder how it will end between Matthew and Mary," she finally said.

Nate stepped closer and lifted her face with his finger under her chin. "It's a script. I can end it however I want."

She swallowed. "End it happily, Nate. That's what people want to see."

He stared at her. "Yes, they do."

She held her breath, only releasing it after he withdrew his hand. "It's obvious that you're excited about this project," she said.

"I've talked to three studios in L.A. They all want a look. They seem intrigued by the rehabilitation-love story angle."

*In L.A.* What did she expect? That's where people like Nate lived. Not in Finnegan Cove. "Congratulations," she said. "I'd better go." She looked around the simple room once more and realized she would see it again. But never just like this.

Her attention wandered to a stack of clothes on the easy chair. Men's clothes. Nice pants, a knit shirt. A belt. Socks and sturdy deck shoes.

She hadn't realized she'd been staring until Nate came up behind her and said, "They're for Dad. I'm taking them to Foggy Creek on Friday so he has something to wear when he gets released."

Jenna's heart skipped a beat. Harley still stood between them. He may have become a better man, but he couldn't erase his past. "Of course," she said. "My mother is planning to be there, too."

"I thought she would." He looked down at Jenna solemnly. "He really loves her, and would never hurt her. My father is reformed."

She rose to her feet and headed for the door. "I really have to go."

"Jenna, please…won't you stay?"

Her hand on the knob, she turned to look at him. His smile was warm, inviting and sincere. She closed her eyes, knowing that if she stared any longer, her heart would betray her. But then he was beside her, touching her face, and in a voice hoarse with emotion, he said, "Jenna, I need to tell you—"

The sound of tires on gravel startled them both. Breaking the contact, Jenna opened the door and looked out. "Your pizza's here," she said.

"I don't give a damn about the pizza."

She crossed the threshold. "I have to go."

"Jenna, wait."

She stopped, staring straight ahead at the plastic pizza shop sign on top of the small car.

"I love you," Nate said as the car door opened.

She stifled a sob.

"Hey, Jenna," said the delivery boy as he strode up. "What's happening?"

"Hi, Bobby." Her head down, she kept walking. *Damned if I know.*

JENNA'S ALARM went off at five-thirty on Friday morning, as usual. Only today she wasn't going to the shop. Neither was Marion. Her mother had asked her friend Bea to fill in for her. She didn't know that last night Jenna had called Shirley and asked her to come in early. Neither mother nor daughter would be at the bakery.

Jenna showered and dressed and left her house an hour later. She arrived at Marion's at seven o'clock, two hours before Harley was scheduled to be released. She found Marion sitting at her kitchen table, dressed in new pastel slacks and a spring print blouse. Her makeup was flawless, her hair freshly colored.

Marion looked up from her coffee. "Jenna. Is something wrong at the shop? Why are you here?"

"I'm here because I was hoping to wrangle an invitation to go with you this morning."

Marion blinked several times and slowly stood. "Oh, sweetheart, are you sure?"

"Yep, I am. If this has a chance of working out, you and I are going to pull together. I know Nate will be there, too."

Marion brushed a tear from under her eye. "I swear, Jenna, you're going to ruin my mascara." She folded her in a hug. When she drew back, she smoothed her hand down Jenna's hair. "I love you,

you know that? I can only imagine what courage it took for you to make this decision, and I promise you, honey, it's going to be okay."

"Harley makes you happy, Mom. I could see that on Sunday." She laughed softly. "I don't know what the holidays are going to be like around here with you, me, Gran and Harley, but if you want him carving the turkey, I'll still bring the cranberry sauce."

Marion squeezed her hand. "And maybe Nate will do the dishes."

Jenna looked away. "I don't think you can count on that, Mom."

Marion gave her an understanding smile. "He loves you. All things are possible."

"Even if that were true," Jenna said, "we live two thousand miles apart."

Marion took her coffee cup to the sink. "You know, sweetheart, I hear there are flights between here and California every day."

ON THE WAY to Foggy Creek, Jenna felt like a pin cushion in a sewing circle, her nerves were so on edge. Her anxiety was directed at seeing Nate, however, not his father.

He'd said he loved her. She loved him. Now what?

How would Nate react when he saw her in the parking lot? Would he resent her interference at this private family moment? Would he question her sudden change of heart, and call it too little, too late? At eight forty-five, she pulled into a parking space.

*One day at a time*, she said to herself. Only this was the day she was putting the rest of her life on the line. For Marion. For Harley. And mostly for Nate. She and Valerie had had a late dinner last night. Afterward, they'd walked down Main Street, and Jenna had confessed that she was afraid of being hurt, and uncertain about the future. But about her feelings for Nate she'd been absolutely clear.

## CHAPTER EIGHTEEN

CRANING HIS NECK and smoothing the knit collar of his new shirt, Harley stared into the dingy mirror in the visitors' restroom. "How do I look?"

Nate stood back and really studied his dad. This wasn't a time for meaningless platitudes or insincere compliments. "You could be an executive getting ready to tee off on the first hole," he said.

Harley chuckled. "Nate, I wasn't any good at golf even before all this."

"Doesn't matter. With that grin on your face, you'd convince them all you're a scratch player."

Harley wrapped his arm around Nate's shoulder. "Well, then, let's get going. I don't want anything to take that grin away."

Nate handed him a simple yellow envelope with his name on the front. "Here are the personal items you had when you checked in. Maybe you'd better take a look at what's inside."

Harley dumped the contents next to the sink and stared down at a billfold, a pair of cracked sunglasses and a ragged menu from a Finnegan Cove bar that had gone out of business. He picked up his old wallet and opened the section that held bills. "Look at this, Nate. I had six bucks when I came in here and it's still inside." He removed a few plastic cards from a slit. "I don't guess I can use a driver's license from two decades ago. And I don't think my old voter registration card is any good."

He slipped the two bills into his pocket and returned the remaining items to the envelope. On his way out, he tossed everything into the garbage can. "It's time to start over, son. New clothes, new life. There's nothing in Foggy Creek I want to take with me."

They left the bathroom and walked to the entrance, where several guards had gathered. They wished Harley well and kidded about how they'd miss him. And then, with his hand in the middle of his father's back, Nate ushered him into the sunshine.

They'd taken only a few steps before Nate saw Marion in the parking lot. When she noticed them, she gave a whoop of such spontaneous jubilation, Nate wished he could have recorded it as a sound bite for a future film project. And then he saw that she wasn't alone. Jenna stood with her hip against her Jeep, her arms folded.

She watched them approach, her expression unreadable as Marion hurried across the lot and threw herself into Harley's arms. He picked her up and twirled her around, and they both laughed. Marion buried her face in the crook of his neck and whispered words meant only for him.

Nate kept his eyes averted and walked around them, not wanting to intrude. When he was within a few feet of Jenna, he raised his head, but couldn't come up with anything to say. He didn't want to jump to an incorrect conclusion. Maybe she'd come along to protect her mother from big, bad Harley. Nate didn't really believe that, and hoped to hell it wasn't so. "It's nice of you to come, I think," he finally said.

She glanced over at Marion and Harley. "Mom's waited twenty years for this. I figured I could invest a couple of hours. Besides, I think your dad could use another person in his official welcoming party."

Nate allowed the first ray of hope to escape his tightly wound self-control. "I expect your support will have a positive effect on Dad's return to Finnegan Cove," he said with a grin. "I know I wouldn't want to tangle with the two Malloy women."

Silence stretched between them until Nate fixed her with a steady gaze and said, "Is that the only reason you're here—moral support?"

She shook her head. It was all he could do not to brush her sun-dappled hair out of her eyes. "Nope. I had to find out what's happening between Matthew and Mary."

"You mean, has she forgiven him for his choices and for generally behaving like an ass?"

"Exactly." Jenna's lips twitched. "I don't know that I'd exactly describe Matthew that way. I'm sure he had his reasons for keeping the truth from Mary."

"At the time he thought he did," Nate said. "Now he just wants her to give him a chance to make it up to her." He stared into Jenna's beautiful green eyes and saw his hope reflected there. He sensed that the next few moments could change the rest of his life. "What do you think, Jenna? What should I do with Mary and Matthew?"

Her smile melted his heart. "For heaven's sake, Nate, do I have to spell it out for you? I'm here today to suggest the perfect ending for your script—one filled with hope and forgiveness and letting go of the past."

He reached down and took her hand. "Does this mean you forgive me?"

She stood on her toes and pressed a kiss to his lips. "I figure if Mary can forgive Matthew, I ought to be able to get over an insignificant thing like you buying a lighthouse for your dad."

"I should have told you everything from the beginning."

"Oh, no doubt about it." She wrapped her hand around his neck and was just pulling his face down to hers again when Nate saw a woman and two children making their way through the parked cars. The woman, tall with brown hair, smiled at him. She kept walking until she got to Harley. Nate and Jenna moved close enough to hear her.

"Can I help you?" Harley asked.

"Are you Harley?"

"Yes."

She stuck out her hand, and he shook it. "My name is Wendy Shelton. I'm your daughter-in-law."

Harley's face split in a huge grin. "Well, I'll be…" He looked at first one child, then the other. "Then these two are…" His voice hitched.

Wendy stepped back. "Say hi to your grandpa," she told them. She started to give Harley their names. With her hand on top of the boy's head, she said, "This is—"

"Brian," Harley stated, grasping his hand. "And Lauren."

The kids smiled, a shy greeting, but Nate knew their reactions would become more natural as the months and years passed. Harley and Marion immediately began asking them questions about school, hobbies, favorite things, while Nate introduced himself and Jenna to Wendy. "Thanks for coming today," he said. "You have no idea what this means to Dad."

"It was the thing to do," she said.

He asked the tough question. "What about Mike?"

She shook her head. "Not here. But he knew I was coming. And he didn't fight me. I think he'll come around."

Nate believed her.

She wished Harley luck and promised to bring the children to visit him.

"Are you really living in a lighthouse?" Brian asked.

"Looks like it," Harley said.

"That's cool."

"Yes, it is. Really cool. I can't wait for you to see it." He smiled at Marion. "And I just happen to know a lady who makes really great cookies."

Wendy took the children's hands, introducing them to Nate and Jenna before she walked back toward her car.

Nate wrapped his arm around Jenna. "Wow, can you believe that?"

"This is a day of new beginnings," she said.

He pulled her close. "Right. Where were we on our new beginning?"

"You were about to apologize—again," she said. "But you need to think of another way to do it."

"Sweetheart, I already have. But I suspect it's going to take me a good long while to get the job done. Maybe all night."

"I have time."

He kissed her thoroughly in the cool shade of the stone walls of Foggy Creek Prison, blessed with the knowledge that four people would soon be taking the first steps into a bright future.

# *EPILOGUE*

NATE SAT IN THE LAST ROW of folding chairs set up in the renovated parlor of the keeper's cottage. He watched his wife at the podium, conducting the meeting of the Finnegan Cove Light Society. Jenna looked adorable in a rust-colored sweater that provided ample room for the gentle swell of her belly. Four and a half months to go. With luck, their son would be a snow baby, a nice bonus for Nate, who'd be spending his first winter in Finnegan Cove in a long time.

Twenty people had come out for this meeting. Some had donated funds toward the final restoration and purchase of the station. Some were there to volunteer their time as guides and caretakers once the light was opened to visitors next week. A sign on the wall behind Jenna proclaimed that the Sean O'Hanlon Lighthouse Museum contained relics from the town's lumbering past, as well as lots of light station memorabilia.

Laughter wafted through the open window. Nate glanced outside at the picnic tables and the lush new lawn, which would eventually become Hester MacDonald Park. Hester was here today, sitting in a lawn chair in her wide-brimmed hat. A dozen children ran out of the woods carrying baskets filled with autumn leaves and pine cones. Wendy was keeping them in line.

Nate, sitting next to Mike, sighed with contentment. "Thanks for the hard work helping Dad and me fix the place up."

Mike shrugged. "Gotta say, Harley's been a valuable addition to Shelton Contracting."

Everyone had been shocked when Mike hired his dad. Mike still called him Harley, not that it mattered. The strides the two had made were more important than what they called each other.

"Sorry you didn't come out too well on this deal," Mike added. "Buying the station for eighty thousand and selling it a few months later for the same amount."

Nate chuckled. "That's okay. At least the Michigan Beacon Society granted the local group enough money for a sizable down payment. Now meeting the mortgage won't be too difficult."

Mike pointed to Harley and Marion, who stood behind a refreshment table loaded with Cove Bakery goodies and apple cider. "Take a look at those two," he said. "They look like poster kids for marriage."

Nate smiled and glanced over at Jenna. He couldn't be more proud of his wife. She'd eventually have to cut down her hours at the hospital, when her pregnancy progressed, but she was determined to be back to work full time as soon as possible. A nursery was in the planning stage at the bakery, so their little guy could spend time with his grandmother and half the town.

Jenna called for questions. One of the more unlikely volunteers, Jubal Payne, asked, "When are they going to start making the movie?"

"I'll defer that question to my husband," Jenna said.

Nate stood. "A production company will be here in ten days." He'd been delighted when the studio had elected to film much of *The Redemption of Matthew Stone* in Finnegan Cove. Everyone was looking forward to an influx of revenue from the filmmakers, and eventual tourist dollars.

Jenna fielded a few more questions before adjourning the meeting. Volunteers crowded around the refreshment table, while Jenna joined Nate. He put his arm around her. "Good job, madam chairwoman."

"The grand opening is going to be wonderful," she said. "I'm so looking forward to it."

"Me, too," he said, "but mostly I'm looking forward to tonight, when all these people will be gone and you and I can sneak back on the grounds."

She smiled.

He placed his hand over her stomach. "I'll bring the soda and the country music."

"And I'll supply the four-wheel-drive Jeep." Jenna kissed his cheek.

The two of them often went into the woods to admire the view from the shore of Lake Michigan. But at night, when the sun went down, they went there just for fun.

\* \* \* \* \*

Look for LAST WOLF WATCHING
by Rhyannon Byrd—the exciting conclusion in the
**BLOODRUNNERS** miniseries
from Silhouette Nocturne.


Follow Michaela and Brody on their fierce journey
to find the truth and face the demons from the past,
as they reach the heart of the battle between the
Runners and the rogues.


Here is a sneak preview of book three,
LAST WOLF WATCHING.

Michaela squinted, struggling to see through the impenetrable darkness. Everyone looked toward the Elders, but she knew Brody Carter still watched her. Michaela could feel the power of his gaze. Its heat. Its strength. And something that felt strangely like anger, though he had no reason to have any emotion toward her. Strangers from different worlds, brought together beneath the heavy silver moon on a night made for hell itself. That was their only connection.

The second she finished that thought, she knew it was a lie. But she couldn't deal with it now. Not tonight. Not when her whole world balanced on the edge of destruction.

Willing her backbone to keep her upright, Michaela Doucet focused on the towering blaze of a roaring bonfire that rose from the far side of the clearing, its orange flames burning with maniacal zeal against the inky black curtain of the night. Many of the Lycans had already shifted into their preternatural shapes, their fur-covered bodies standing like monstrous shadows at the edges of the forest as they waited with restless expectancy for her brother.

Her nineteen-year-old brother, Max, had been attacked by a rogue werewolf—a Lycan who preyed upon humans for food. Max had been bitten in the attack, which meant he was no longer human, but a breed of creature that existed between the two worlds of man and beast, much like the Bloodrunners themselves.

The Elders parted, and two hulking shapes emerged from the trees. In their wolf forms, the Lycans stood over seven feet tall, their legs bent at an odd angle as they stalked forward. They each held a thick chain that had been wound around their inside wrists, the twin lengths leading back into the shadows. The Lycans had taken no more than a few steps when they jerked on the chains, and her brother appeared.

Bound like an animal.

Biting at her trembling lower lip, she glanced left, then right, surprised to see that others had joined her. Now the Bloodrunners and their family and friends stood as a united force against the Silvercrest pack, which had yet to accept the fact that something sinister was eating away at its foundation—something that would rip down the protective walls that separated their world from the humans'. It occurred to Michaela that loyalties were being announced tonight—a separation made between those who would stand with the Runners in their fight against the rogues and those who blindly supported the pack's refusal to face reality. But all she could focus on was her brother. Max looked so hurt…so terrified.

"Leave him alone," she screamed, her soft-soled, black satin slip-ons struggling for purchase in the damp earth as she rushed toward Max, only to find herself lifted off the ground when a hard, heavily muscled arm clamped around her waist from behind, pulling her clear off her feet. "Damn it, let me down!" she snarled, unable to take her eyes off her brother as the golden-eyed Lycan kicked him.

Mindless with heartache and rage, Michaela clawed at the arm holding her, kicking her heels against whatever part of her captor's legs she could reach. "Stop it," a deep, husky voice grunted in her ear. "You're not helping him by losing it. I give you my word he'll survive the ceremony, but you have to keep it together."

"Nooooo!" she screamed, too hysterical to listen to reason. "You're monsters! All of you! Look what you've done to him! How dare you! *How dare you!*"

The arm tightened with a powerful flex of muscle, cinching her waist. Her breath sucked in on a sharp, wailing gasp.

"Shut up before you get both yourself and your brother killed. I will *not* let that happen. Do you understand me?" her captor growled, shaking her so hard that her teeth clicked together. "Do you understand me, Doucet?"

"Damn it," she cried, stricken as she watched one

of the guards grab Max by his hair. Around them Lycans huffed and growled as they watched the spectacle, while others outright howled for the show to begin.

"That's enough!" the voice seethed in her ear. "They'll tear you apart before you even reach him, and I'll be damned if I'm going to stand here and watch you die."

Suddenly, through the haze of fear and agony and outrage in her mind, she finally recognized who'd caught her. *Brody.*

He held her in his arms, her body locked against his powerful form, her back to the burning heat of his chest. A low, keening sound of anguish tore through her, and her head dropped forward as hoarse sobs of pain ripped from her throat. "Let me go. I have to help him. *Please,*" she begged brokenly, knowing only that she needed to get to Max. "Let me go, Brody."

He muttered something against her hair, his breath warm against her scalp, and Michaela could have sworn it was a single word…. But she must have heard wrong. She was too upset. Too furious. Too terrified. She must be out of her mind.

Because it sounded as if he'd quietly snarled the word *never*.

# nocturne™

### THE FINAL INSTALLMENT OF
### THE BLOODRUNNERS TRILOGY

## Last Wolf Watching

Runner Brody Carter has found his match in
Michaela Doucet, a human with unusual psychic powers.
When Michaela's brother is threatened, Brody becomes
her protector, and suddenly not only has to protect her
from her enemies but also from himself....

**LOOK FOR**

# LAST WOLF WATCHING
## BY

# RHYANNON
# BYRD

*Available May 2008 wherever you buy books.*

**Dramatic and Sensual Tales of Paranormal Romance**

www.eHarlequin.com          SN61786

# HARLEQUIN® *Romance*®

## Western Weddings

Jason Welborn was convinced that his business partner's daughter, Jenny, had come to claim her share in the business. But Jenny seemed determined to win him over, and the more he tried to push her away, the more feisty Jenny's response. Slowly but surely she was starting to get under Jason's skin....

*Look for*

# Coming Home to the Cattleman

*by*

# JUDY CHRISTENBERRY

*Available May wherever you buy books.*

## HARLEQUIN®
### *Live the emotion*™

**www.eHarlequin.com**

HRI7511

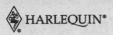

# INTRIGUE

Introducing

## THE CURSE OF RAVEN'S CLIFF

A quaint seaside village's most chilling secrets are revealed for the first time in this new continuity!

Britta Jackobson disappeared from the witness protection program without a trace. But could Ryan Burton return Britta to safety—when the most dangerous thing in her life was him?

Look for

## WITH THE MATERIAL WITNESS IN THE SAFEHOUSE

### BY CARLA CASSIDY

Available May 2008 wherever you buy books.

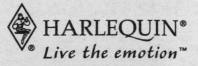

HARLEQUIN®

*Live the emotion™*

# REQUEST YOUR FREE BOOKS!

## 2 FREE NOVELS PLUS 2 FREE GIFTS!

HARLEQUIN®

*Super Romance®*

### Exciting, emotional, unexpected!

**YES!** Please send me 2 FREE Harlequin Superromance® novels and my 2 FREE gifts (gifts are worth about $10). After receiving them, if I don't wish to receive any more books, I can return the shipping statement marked "cancel." If I don't cancel, I will receive 6 brand-new novels every month and be billed just $4.69 per book in the U.S. or $5.24 per book in Canada, plus 25¢ shipping and handling per book and applicable taxes, if any*. That's a savings of close to 15% off the cover price! I understand that accepting the 2 free books and gifts places me under no obligation to buy anything. I can always return a shipment and cancel at any time. Even if I never buy another book from Harlequin, the two free books and gifts are mine to keep forever.

135 HDN EEX7    336 HDN EEYK

| Name | (PLEASE PRINT) | |
|------|------|------|
| Address | | Apt. # |
| City | State/Prov. | Zip/Postal Code |

Signature (if under 18, a parent or guardian must sign)

### Mail to the Harlequin Reader Service:
**IN U.S.A.:** P.O. Box 1867, Buffalo, NY 14240-1867
**IN CANADA:** P.O. Box 609, Fort Erie, Ontario L2A 5X3

Not valid to current subscribers of Harlequin Superromance books.

### Want to try two free books from another line?
### Call 1-800-873-8635 or visit www.morefreebooks.com.

* Terms and prices subject to change without notice. N.Y. residents add applicable sales tax. Canadian residents will be charged applicable provincial taxes and GST. This offer is limited to one order per household. All orders subject to approval. Credit or debit balances in a customer's account(s) may be offset by any other outstanding balance owed by or to the customer. Please allow 4 to 6 weeks for delivery. Offer available while quantities last.

**Your Privacy:** Harlequin is committed to protecting your privacy. Our Privacy Policy is available online at www.eHarlequin.com or upon request from the Reader Service. From time to time we make our lists of customers available to reputable third parties who may have a product or service of interest to you. If you would prefer we not share your name and address, please check here. ☐

HSR08

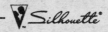

# SPECIAL EDITION™

## THE WILDER FAMILY
### Healing Hearts in Walnut River

Social worker Isobel Suarez was proud to
work at Walnut River General Hospital, so
when Neil Kane showed up from the attorney
general's office to investigate insurance fraud,
she was up in arms. Until she melted in his
arms, and things got very tricky...

Look for

# HER MR. RIGHT?

by

# *KAREN ROSE SMITH*

*Available May wherever books are sold.*

# HARLEQUIN® *Super Romance*®

# COMING NEXT MONTH

**#1488 A SMALL-TOWN TEMPTATION • Terry McLaughlin**
When acquisitions specialist Jack Maguire arrives in Charlie Keene's small town, nobody's safe. Not Charlie and not the family business she's desperate to keep from this Southern charmer...

**#1489 THE MAN BEHIND THE COP • Janice Kay Johnson**
*Count on a Cop*
Detective Bruce Walker has vowed never to get involved, never to risk emotional entanglements. But then he meets Karin Jorgenson, and the attraction is so intense, he risks breaking his promise. Can he trust himself enough to show her the real man inside?

**#1490 ANYTHING FOR HER CHILDREN • Darlene Gardner**
*Suddenly a Parent*
Raising someone else's children has tested Keri Cassidy, so when trouble strikes too close to home she's quick to meet the challenge. Although sorting out her adopted son's basketball coach seems easy pickin's, she soon finds out there's a lot more to the gorgeous, quiet man—there's a scandal in Grady Quinlan's past. But the spark between him and Keri may be exactly what it takes to start a new future for them all....

**#1491 HIS SECRET PAST • Ellen Hartman**
*Single Father*
If she can only make one more film, it's got to count. And award-winning documentary filmmaker Anna Walsh knows exactly what she has to do. Track down the former lead singer of the rock band Five Star and make him tell her what happened the night her best friend died.

**#1492 BABY BY CONTRACT • Debra Salonen**
*Spotlight on Sentinel Pass*
Libby McGannon's ad for a donor lands actor Cooper Lindstrom, and she's thrilled. With his DNA, her baby will be gorgeous! While this is a business exchange, her feelings are unbusinesslike...until she discovers his real reasons for being in Sentinel Pass.

**#1493 HIDDEN LEGACY • Margaret Way**
*Everlasting Love*
When Alyssa Sutherland's great-aunt Zizi dies unexpectedly, Alyssa inherits her beautiful house in Australia's north Queensland. But Zizi's legacy also includes a secret.... It's Zizi's friend and neighbor, the handsome young architect Adam Hunt, who helps Alyssa reveal the love her aunt kept hidden all those years.